IDENTITY
OF
DEATH

An Arkansas River Valley Mystery

BERYL WEALAND

BERYL WEALAND

IDENTITY
OF
DEATH

An Arkansas River Valley Mystery

A Novel

Pairodocs

RUSSELLVILLE & DOVER, ARKANSAS

D
DOC
C

Pairodocs
37 Gilbert Lane, Dover, AR 72837
479-967-9568
Pairodocs

ISBN: 978-0-9990630-2-6 (sc)
ISBN: 978-0-9990630-3-3 (e)

Library of Congress Control Number: 2018912719

Lulu Publishing Services rev. date: 10/30/2018

DEDICATION

This book is dedicated to our friends who are ageing
with dignity, no matter what the circumstances

1

Addison Douglas Daniels, known locally as Uncle ADD, did not like digging holes. In fact, he hated it as much as trips to the VA hospital in Little Rock. The dry rocky soil of the Ozarks could flat wear a man out. The only reason he had agreed to be the shovel man was because of the moonstone. And just as he needed the cancer therapies of the VA, he needed the promise of treasure from the moonstone.

ADD's old friend, Raymond Bailey had recently come into possession of a moonstone, and he and ADD had been digging holes all over creation for the last two months. ADD didn't know how Raymond had come by a moonstone. The local lore was that it was meant to belong to the seventh son of a seventh son. Raymond's father had been a seventh son, true, but Raymond had six sisters, so technically he didn't qualify.

ADD figured the proof was in the pudding, and twice the moonstone had brought treasure, if you could call it that. The moonstone was a seer's stone. You held it at chest height and turned your back to the moon so that the light came over your right shoulder. Then the stone lit up and showed where lost objects like rings, or even coins, were buried beneath the leaves. It was better than a metal detector because it could find objects wrapped in cloth or inside a wooden box. Because the light had to be just right, the moonstone could be used only three nights a month, the night of the full moon and the nights before and after. Cloud cover, rain, or fog pretty well wiped out any of your chances with a moonstone.

I

Last month ADD had dug a half-dozen holes, but only one was a strike. They had found an old piece of chewing tobacco wrapped in a handkerchief inside a rotting cigar box about two feet down. ADD was sore for a week! Almost any place on a hill around here was good for rocks or hardpan about six inches down. If Raymond hadn't been so insistent, ADD would have stopped at one foot down for sure. Then last night, the night just before the full moon, they had dug up an old, rotten leather bridle with a rusted snaffle bit.

2

Tonight there were three of them on the hunt. ADD, his girlfriend, Beulah Lamb, and Raymond were crowded onto the bench seat of ADD's pickup. The moon was on the rise, and should be just about at its peak by the time they reached their destination, the old Galley Rock Cemetery.

Beulah did not enjoy being sandwiched between the two men, or, to be more precise, she didn't like sitting next to Raymond. He didn't bathe regularly, and the odor of his breath suggested he hadn't brushed his teeth since Moses came down from the mountain. Add to that the odor of his goats and the manure on his shoes and pants, and Beulah was having a hard time keeping from gagging. But this trip was at her request, so the least she could do was be nice to **Mr.** Bailey.

You see, Beulah had her own kind of "seeing". She saw dead people. And, from time-to-time they gave her messages. Most of the messages were useless because most of the people were at least a hundred years old. Like the time Abraham Lincoln had warned her that he planned to free the slaves in Arkansas, and that she needed to be extremely cautious around anybody suspected of being a member of the KKK since northern sympathizers were as vulnerable as black folk. But this new message had been more direct. This message was from Jesse James.

Jesse James had been dead since 1882, but his legend was well known in the River Valley. It seems Jesse, Frank and unidentified members of the James-Younger gang passed through from time to time on their way to Hot

Springs. Perhaps Jesse took the baths to ease his numerous wounds. He had been near death from chest wounds on at least two occasions before the death shot. But it was well known that he couldn't resist a little gambling, and the 20th Century reputation of Hot Springs had started in the late 1800's.

There were stories of Jesse James sightings in the Pottsville and Norristown (now Russellville) area. Down along the river between the two towns, a large corner post bore the initials JJ, neatly shot into the wood. And, the story is told that one evening, three men on tired horses rode up to a farm house near the river asking for room and meals for one night. The older couple living there figured that the three were none other than Jesse, Frank, and Cole Younger. They accommodated the trio, feeding them, taking care of their horses, and giving them a reasonable bed to sleep in. The next morning after breakfast, Jesse offered the woman a $20-dollar gold piece which she politely refused. The couple was grateful they had enough to accommodate passersby on their way across the river. Then Jesse offered her a beautiful gold ring. She knew the gang had begun robbing trains and their passengers, so she refused the ill-gotten gain. The well from the farm is still visible just up the hill from Vinsons Electric on HWY-7 just north of the Arkansas River bridge.

Jesse had told Beulah to go to the cemetery because she needed to find something there. He was vague about just what it was, but he had been very specific that it was located somewhere between the last tombstone and the big oak at the end of the cemetery. Beulah was nobody's fool (most of the time). She couldn't believe that her mind was making up such nonsense for her to dream about, so she dismissed the dream. But Jesse was persistent; he appeared three times as young Jesse with his bright blue eyes, not the heavier, bearded Jesse who had been shot by a member of his own gang.

Beulah toyed with the idea of finding something in that old cemetery and woolied it back and forth in her mind until she convinced herself that the younger Jesse had indeed left something out there at Galley Rock. It couldn't be metal. Folks with metal detectors had pretty well scoured all the old cemeteries in the state. It might be cash, but Confederate bills weren't worth anything now (as if they had ever been). Nevertheless the idea of buried treasure weighed on her mind until she had confided in ADD.

"Addie," she approached him at breakfast, "I've been havin' some strange dreams."

Uh oh, ADD thought to himself. *That explains the pecan pancakes in the middle of the week.* He gave her his full attention and nodded for her to continue.

"Well," she was a little sheepish, "I've been seein' Jesse James for the past several nights. He says there's something I need to go get down there at that old Galley Rock Cemetery south of Atkins"

"And just what might that something be?" ADD was skeptical.

"Oh my," she sighed, "he didn't say. But he was very clear about where it is. He said to look between the last tombstone and the giant oak there at the end of the gravestones. What do you think it could be? Maybe he left something from one of his robberies. It might be worth a lot."

Now ADD was known to be one of the smartest men in the area (all those Daniels were smart), but he was also known to exhibit "eccentric" behavior. Some said he had a few screws loose, and others cut to the chase and said he was just plumb goofy!

Uncle ADD talked to the Lord Almighty every day. ADD truly believed that he had been led directly to Beulah Lamb there at the sheep pens at the Pope County fair. So, although he couldn't understand the logic of it, he pledged his cooperation when the Lord Almighty told him to humor Beulah. Once again, ADD agreed to do all the digging if Raymond would help them locate the spot with his moonstone.

Raymond was not inclined to cooperate. It was his moonstone, and he made all the calls about where to look for treasure. "Well, I don't know," he whined. "It could be that there's somethin' there. But that's a mighty far piece ta go, and I jus' think we ought ta stay up this way. There's a full moon a comin', an' I've got in mind some new places ta look."

ADD had known Raymond for many a year, and he figured the man just wanted to be begged. So he had begged. The result was a late foray last night, the night before the full moon, and tonight was cemetery night!

3

The first problem the three encountered was finding the cemetery. They passed it several times before stopping at a large historic marker for Galley Rock. As they looked around they realized they were practically at the cemetery. It was downhill from the marker about 40 feet. A horseshoe shaped metal arc with the words, Galley Rock, sheltered a chain link fence with a locked double gate and an open single gate for pedestrian entry.

The cemetery was no longer in use and was beginning to show neglect. Knee high weeds and grass intermingled with volunteer briars covered most of the ground. Come spring, a cleanup crew would cut and rake the browned vegetation, and the tombstones would be easier to find. The three slowly wended their way up the steep hill toward the trees on the left side of the lot. There they met their second problem. There was no large oak tree. Beulah and Raymond waited while ADD checked the nearby boundaries. He encountered several small oaks, three large hickories, and any number of large catalpas. Jesse's memory may have been good after 130 or so years, but he had no clue about tornadoes and fires that had swept through the area since then.

The full moon was approaching its nightly zenith, so the three decided to make a try with the moonstone since it had to be more accurate than Jesse's obsolete directions. Beulah and ADD stayed out of the way while Raymond began his ritual. He stomped his way south toward the center of the cemetery next to a very old headstone and turned his back to the moon as he cupped the egg-shaped, opalescent stone in both his hands and held it away from his body until he could see reflected moon light. Then he continued to the south, the direction opposite of where they had expected to be looking. Granted, it was a bit of a surprise, but then what could Jesse James possibly know about the current layout of the graves?

Raymond worked his way back across the graveyard, stopping near different headstones to check his moonstone. The cemetery was on a high hill with lots of rocks and rough places to trip on, not to mention the old grave markers that were almost invisible in the dark. ADD and Beulah sighed with resignation, then picked up the post-hole digger and long handled spade and trailed along. They had crossed most of the cemetery running north-south when Raymond finally stopped at what appeared to be a family plot with three large and several small headstones enclosed in a wrought iron fence about five feet tall.

"There's somethin' in there," Raymond pointed to the enclosure.

"Yeah," retorted the frustrated ADD, "there's a bunch of tombstones in there."

"Now, now, don't go a gettin' testy on me. It's over there between the big headstone and the little one just past it. I seen it with tha moonstone."

"What did you see?" ADD wanted to know.

"Well, I ain't certain. It looks like a bunch of stuff. But it's there fer sure."

ADD groaned out loud. "You mean we got to get inside to do our diggin'?"

"Yep, ya cain't dig from out here."

ADD propped the post-hole digger against the fence then walked around the enclosure trying all the sections and the chained gate, trying to find a way in. No luck. He sighed again with his hands on his hips. Then he walked all the way back to the chained gate where he had parked and fiddled with the lock until it released. He crawled into his truck and drove it very carefully to near the iron fence around the plot, then backed slowly until his tailgate was almost touching the fence.

"Come on, Beulah, if we got to do this. I'll go over first then help you." He lifted the digging tools over the fence first. Then he helped Beulah up into the truck bed and climbed up too. The tail gate was sitting about a foot from the top of the fence, so he climbed up and over using the fence to break his fall. Then Beulah did the same thing while ADD grabbed her butt and helped her down.

Once inside they gathered the tools and moved between the two tombstones. There was plenty of room, meaning it was very likely someone from the family would be buried here later. The full moon was really bright now, and the two didn't have any trouble marking off a rectangle to dig in. They started at the center and worked out. ADD would have a go with the post-hole digger then Beulah would move the dirt aside with the shovel.

The digging here was easy compared with digging in rocks. The grass had been kept down, and the dirt might even have been tilled during the last year of two. Then they found it. Beulah held the flashlight as ADD carefully uncovered a black trash bag tightly sealed with duct tape. "Is that it?" ADD asked Raymond who was sitting in the front seat of the truck swinging his feet.

Raymond made a big show of consulting his moonstone before replying. "Yep, that's it. I told you it was more than one thing!" He was clearly proud of himself.

The next problem ADD and Beulah faced was getting out. They handed the tools and the plastic bags up to Raymond who had moved to the bed of the truck. Now, how to get themselves out. There wasn't anything for them to crawl up on to get over the fence. Finally ADD hatched a plan.

"Beulah," he asked, "how far can you step up without losing your balance?"

Beulah hiked her leg up a few times to test it. "I'd say about two feet if I stretch it."

"That should do it. Raymond, pull the spare tire out of the well. Now tie that piece of rope around it and lower it over the fence." They lowered the tire and tied it into place with the bottom of the wheel about 18 inches above the ground. "Now hook the end of that come-along onto the tie-down hook there in the bed. Throw the rest of it down to me." ADD grasped the come-along and used it to steady himself while he stepped onto the bottom of the wheel rim, then onto the top of the tire, then over the fence into the truck bed. He made it look easy, as if he were a mountain goat.

It was not so easy for Beulah who was a lamb, not a goat. She slid off the narrow lower edge of the rim several times until she got the hang of using just her toes. Then she pulled against the upper rope and finally made it to the top of the tire where she froze. ADD and Raymond reached over the fence and grabbed her bodily to pull her up and over. Never mind the bruises on her abdomen and her stretched shoulders.

"We got it; we got it!" The two men were hopping up and down with excitement. "Let's open it!"

"No," Beulah argued. "There could be something really nasty in there. Let's take it back to the house where we'll have plenty of light, and water, too, if we need to wash something off."

As soon as the trio drove up to ADD's place, Beulah made a bee line for the bathroom, barely making it with just a few dribbles onto her safety pad. ADD and Raymond were content to pee off the end of the porch. Somehow their simultaneous streams sealed their partnership. As Beulah raised her shirt to look in the mirror at the bruises on her abdomen from being dragged across the iron fence, she wondered, not for the first time, how she had ever engineered this mess.

Beulah went to the kitchen where she set up a pot of Mr. Coffee then pulled several days' newspapers out of the recycle box and spread them in thick layers onto the old oak table. The guys could hardly wait to bring their treasure in and place it gently on the papers. ADD decided to prolong the anticipation by insisting that he have a cup of coffee first to "settle his nerves".

"Would you care for a cup of coffee, Mr. Bailey?" Beulah asked politely, trying to put some distance between them by the use of a more formal address.

"Don't care 'f I do!" he responded in his most polite country vernacular.

Beulah interpreted that to mean that yes, he did care for a cup of coffee. "Do you take anything in it?" she asked as she poured generous mugs for both men.

"Nope. I don't take nothing," he accepted the mug and took a big swig.

Beulah gathered a pair of scissors, a butcher knife, and several black trash bags. She offered yellow kitchen gloves to the men, who declined the offer, then put on a pair herself. The coffee ritual being over, it was time to open the bags.

"Jesse James, here we go!" ADD exclaimed even though he knew perfectly well that Jesse had never seen a black plastic trash bag in his entire life. Raymond still didn't use trash bags, so he was none the wiser. Using the butcher knife, ADD cut the twisted knot off the top of the bag and eased it open. The three literally bumped heads trying to see what was inside.

What was inside was a mystery to all three. There were six identical hard plastic boxes each measuring about 6"x 8"x 1½ ". The boxes were khaki colored and each had a hand-written name on one end. ADD took out his pocket knife to pry one of the boxes open. The lid was very tight, and when it finally came off, some of the box's contents were spilled out onto the table. They were looking at the ashes of a cremated human.

Raymond's face turned white as he squawked an unintelligible sound and jumped up from the table and backed several feet toward the arch connecting the kitchen and living room. "It's the Devil's work! It's the Devil's work! The Devil's done cursed my moonstone!" He took the stone in its bag out of his pocket and slung it through the arch into the living room as if it were burning his hands.

Beulah sat frozen, unsure what to do. Fortunately ADD had the presence of mind to retrieve the bag and run to the front porch where he threw it into the rose bushes, marking the spot in his mind for later.

"I'm afraid you're right," he agreed with Raymond. "But we didn't know we were diggin' up death. That wasn't our intention at all. If we get rid of the ashes and cleanse the moonstone, I'm sure the Lord Almighty will forgive us."

Raymond could see the wisdom of ADD's advice. It'd be a real pity if the moonstone's power were completely lost. "Well," he said, "if yer sure that'll take care of it. I reckon we could give 'er a try. But I ain't touchin' them bones. Yer the one who opened thet box, an' it's you whose soul is in danger of eternal damnation."

"Now don't you go a worryin' about me," ADD soothed. "You go on home now, and I'll take care of the bones. We'll leave the moonstone where it is until the dark of the moon passes. By then the Devil will have found himself another victim to bother. I'll be askin' the Good Lord to cleanse that stone every day, and if anything changes, I'll come over and tell you myself."

When ADD went back into the house, he found Beulah in her own recliner sipping a cup of coffee. He went to the kitchen and refilled his own mug then joined her. "Did you get him settled down? I like to have had a heart attack, him jumpin' up that way!" she complained.

"Yeah, I think he's calmed down now. I told him I'd get rid of the bones and we'd leave the moonstone under the rose bushes during the dark of the moon. He'll come around. He likes bossing me around too much to give up on it completely."

Beulah giggled as she recognized the truth. Still she did feel just a little guilty for leading them into the situation. If she ever saw that damned Jesse James again, she'd tell him a thing or two!

"ADD," she asked earnestly, "do you have any idea what those boxes were doin' out there in that cemetery? Somebody hid them there deliberately. Those boxes should have gone to relatives, or to a rest garden. It just isn't right."

"No," he was thinking out loud, "I have to admit that this is a real puzzler. I sure hope we're not breaking any laws havin' those bones here. I don't have much experience with scatterin' ashes and such. But I know someone who does. We'll take these over to Garnet. They handle stuff like this at the Med School all the time. I bet she'll know exactly what to do."

5

Dr. Garnet Daniels was having a particularly pleasant day. She loved teaching Human Gross Anatomy for the med students at Mt. Nebo State University (MNSU). Today was the first lab, the day the students met their cadavers for the first time. Fifty students had started this morning. Now it was time for the second batch of 50 to begin the time honored process.

Students assembled around each table in groups of four, cracking crude jokes and trying not to show their discomfort with actually touching their first cadaver. The dissecting groups would coat their cadaver's face with Vaseline and wrap the head in gauze. This procedure would help keep the facial tissues moist until later in the semester when students had acquired enough skill and finesse to complete the tedious dissection of the face.

But first, the names were read. There was always the possibility that a student might have known a particular cadaver. That cadaver would be removed and exchanged with one that was not known in order to avoid a potentially traumatic experience. The names having been read, all identifiers were removed from the table, and the students began the Vaseline and gauze process.

Garnet was giving group five a little assistance when she heard a sharp intake of breath from Dr. Bradshaw, one of her fellow teachers. When she looked up, Morry Bradshaw's face had become quite pale, and his eyes were glued to the female on the table. He was definitely alarmed! Garnet rushed over to assist Morry. When she saw the cadaver, she looked at Morry, then at the cadaver, then at Morry. As their eyes locked, Garnet's quick thinking helped mobilize him.

"Oh my," she blurted, "we're not supposed to use her. She was selected for the surgeons in-service because she exhibited lymph edema when she died."

"You're right. I knew there was some mix-up," Morry ad-libbed. "Hang on," he addressed the four-student dissecting team. "We'll get you a different cadaver. Damn surgeons are so picky."

Mr. Hartman, the department's embalmer/denier knew that the surgeons were not coming until next week and that they would require a fresh, unembalmed cadaver to practice various surgical approaches. Nevertheless, he sensed Dr. Bradshaw's mild panic and played along. Cadaver five was removed and replaced with another female. With 25 cadavers, the goal was to provide about equal numbers of males and females for the students.

The remainder of the lab progressed as usual. Once the faces were wrapped, the next chore was to place each cadaver in the prone position (face down). The muscles of the back were relatively large, and would survive the misdirected hacking of the novice dissectors. Although the students had been given gloving and safety instructions, Garnet held her breath as she witnessed one aggressive young man use a scalpel to slice away some superficial fascia. He froze as the tips of his gloves fell off, revealing the ends of his fingers mere millimeters away. He took a deep breath, put the scalpel down, and carefully proceeded with dissecting scissors. Lesson learned!

As soon as the last student pushed through the door with his shoulders, holding both hands up and sniffing the unmistakable odor of cadaver, Morry and Garnet made a beeline to the rejected cadaver which Mr. Hartman was uncovering for them.

"It can't be!" Morry burst out.

"But it is. I'd know her anywhere. That's Ella Justice. She worked here five years. And the irony is that she did the secretarial work for the Donated Body Program. How in the world did this happen? What name did she come in under?"

Mr. Hartman held up the donated body papers, "Edna Summermann, with two m's and two n's," he read the name.

Garnet, Dr. Bradshaw, Dr. Simmons (the third instructor for the course), and Mr. Hartman huddled in the embalmer's office. Mr. Hartman pulled the paper file for Edna Summermann. Whoever she was, she had indeed registered with the donated body program. And, Mr. Hartman pulled up the electronic file, so had Ella Justice!

"Well, that's a relief," Morry Bradshaw exhaled audibly. "That means we can go ahead and use the body."

"Not exactly," Mr. Hartman disagreed. "We can't use her until we have a death certificate. That's one of our own regulations."

"Oh," the other three stated in unison.

"Does Edna Summermann have one?" Morry asked.

Mr. Hartman shuffled through the paper file, his expression becoming more sober as he looked, then looked again. "It doesn't appear to be here," he was clearly puzzled. "We're not supposed to take a body without it. Let me see. Looks like David (the night custodian) signed it in."

"Aren't you supposed to be notified when a body comes in?" Garnet was puzzled.

"Yes, but this delivery clearly fell through the cracks, death certificate and all," Mr. Hartman was becoming more alarmed.

"It looks like we have to do two things," Dr. Bradshaw took charge. "First, we'd better tell Forrest" (Dr. Forrest Garrison was the Department Chair). "Then we'd better find out where these bodies, well this one anyway, came from. And, I guess this makes three things, we need to find those death certificates."

The three anatomists kicked around some ideas for a while then decided to start again tomorrow. Morry Bradshaw promised to call the others if anything changed tonight.

Garnet went back to her office for her notes for tomorrow's lecture. She hated giving up her slides and overheads, but the new virtual reality dissection was a great teaching tool. As she drove home, her mind was spinning. How in the world had those two ladies been mixed up? And, where was the real Edna Summermann? Was she even dead?

Hopefully the night custodian would be able to shed some light on the situation.

Garnet was looking forward to a glass of sangria and a talk with Mica, her husband. The day had become more tiring than she had anticipated. Her outlook didn't improve when she saw Uncle ADD's old pickup in the parking area by her house.

Oh lordy, what now? Garnet thought to herself. She loved her Uncle ADD to death, as they say, **but** he could be a real pain in the butt. Whenever he showed up unannounced, there was likely to be a problem, usually some mess he'd gotten himself into. Garnet had her own mess to sort through. The last thing she needed right now was one of Uncle ADD's messes.

Uncle ADD was the last of her father's family. Although he had been born 10 years later than her father, he had still picked up (inherited?) many of the same family quirks. He believed the only book worth studying was the Bible, and he could quote a scripture either for or against almost anything depending on how the wind was blowing. He referred to himself as a "Spiritual Jew" who kept the Sabbath and never ate pork. He prayed obsessively and claimed that the Lord Almighty spoke to him directly to guide his footsteps along life's journey. Needless to say, Garnet wasn't in the mood to deal with him tonight.

After taking several calming breaths, Garnet gathered her briefcase and papers then walked slowly to her own front door. Across the living room, at the big table next to the kitchen, ADD and his latest girlfriend, Beulah, were chatting with Mica. In the middle of the table was a large black trash bag.

"Oh, good. You're home," Mica welcomed her enthusiastically. "ADD and Beulah have found something for you to see. I can't wait to see it myself. Come get something to drink. Then we'll take a look. ADD was just telling me about his friend with the moonstone. They hit pay dirt last night, but they said they couldn't let me see it unless you were here."

"How thoughtful of them," Garnet's tone was a little facetious, but Mica frowned at her, and she checked her attitude. Mica poured her a large glass of tea, and she joined them at the table.

"Hold your hat, 'cause this will knock your socks off," ADD mixed metaphors as he undid the wire twist on one of the bags. He reached in and pulled out two of the boxes of cremains (cremated remains). Then he reached in twice more until he had six boxes lined up on Garnet's table.

Garnet was flabbergasted by the display, and Mica's look was incredulous. For once, both of them were at a loss for words. Garnet recovered first. "Where? Why?" she asked, completely puzzled by the boxes of strangers on her table.

ADD was an old style story teller, so he did the honors, dragging out and embellishing the cemetery adventure. "Now the thing I'm worried about is whether there's legal ramifications on account of us takin' these boxes," he finally concluded.

"I'm not sure what the law is on digging things up in cemeteries," Garnet replied. "I don't think just having possession of these boxes puts you into legal jeopardy, but I will have to look that up on the internet. My main question is: what in the sam hell are you doing running around with a moonstone and digging holes all over the countryside?"

ADD looked a little sheepish while Beulah tried to hide a smirk, perfectly willing to give ADD all the blame for this latest boondoggle. "Well," he admitted, "I'm afraid I'm guilty as charged. I knew that moonstone couldn't be bona fide on account of it only works for the seventh son of a seventh son. Now Raymond is a son, and he is the seventh in his family, but the first six are girls." Mica coughed and turned his head to hide his laughter.

"So you thought you'd just give it a try anyway?" Garnet countered accusingly.

"Yeah, I did. We never found anything to amount to much, not countin' last night. Besides we were havin' more fun than I've had in years, even if I did have to do all the diggin'."

"Anyway," Beulah chipped in, cutting off any further questions. "We were goin' to a movie tonight anyway. So we thought we might as well drop these off with you on our way. You're the one who knows all about dead people after all." She was so nonchalant and cheery, Garnet almost bought into it.

"Well, you two run along then. I'll keep these and look into it sometime this week. I have some meetings scheduled so I can't promise you when. But I'll get back to you." She decided to play nicey-nice just to get rid of them.

When ADD and Beulah had gone, Garnet and Mica looked at each other across the table and burst out laughing. "A moonstone!" Garnet shook her head in disbelief. "I haven't heard about anybody using a moonstone for, let's see, maybe 50 years."

"I know. I almost laughed out loud when he was explaining it to me before you came home. I managed to stifle it though when I saw he was dead serious. But that line about the seventh son of the seventh son really got to me. I nearly choked myself on that one."

They laughed some more as they ate their dinner of ham sandwiches and salad followed by sugar-free ice cream and Oreos. Then Garnet told Mica about today's mix-up at the morgue.

"I don't see what the problem is," Mica offered. "I thought she signed herself up for the donated body program before she left. So now you have the body. What's the problem?"

"The problem is we don't have a death certificate, and we can't use the body until we get one. And, we're not really sure what happened to our other donor. There's no death certificate for her either, and the body could be anywhere."

"So you're pretty sure there's something wrong besides just a mix-up?"

"Oh, I'm definitely sure something's wrong," Garnet was firm. "Here, take a look at this box," she turned one of the boxes of cremains toward Mica so he could read Ella Justice's name on the end.

"How did she get into that box?" Mica was dumbfounded. "You just said…"

"No, she's not in that box. I know exactly where she is. She's in our morgue."

"Then who's in that box?" Mica asked.

"Well, it may be our other donor. That's what I have to find out."

Garnet left the boxes of cremains at home in their garbage bag when she hustled out of the house the next morning at 6:30. She'd deal with them later after she'd learned more about how to dispose of them legally. Today she had an emergency meeting with the department chair, the other Gross Anatomy faculty, and Mr. Hartman.

"Now let me get this straight," Dr. Forrest Garrison summarized. "We have the body of Ella Justice, but the paperwork for a Mrs. Summermann, minus her death certificate. Is that correct? When they all nodded, he continued. "Ella was a body donor, but we can't use her body, or trade it, or even transport it without her death certificate. We have the donor paperwork for Mrs. Summermann, but not her body. Since there has obviously been some kind of mistake, let me call the livery service to find out where the bodies came from initially. Then we'll go from there. Shouldn't be too hard to track down."

Garnet was not surprised when Dr. Garrison came by her office around 11:00. "Well," he began tentatively, "it's getting more complicated. The livery service picked up two bodies from Bach's Funeral Services back in March, one for us, and one to be taken to the crematorium. It would appear that the two bodies were switched in transit. That should be easy to solve except that the livery driver was Johnny Earl Rambo, and the night delivery agent at Bach's was Johnny Joe Rambo."

Oh, no!" Garnet reacted immediately, thumping her forehead with the heel of her hand. "The Johnny twins! That's all we need."

The Johnny twins were dysfunctional cousins from the Rambo family, both named Johnny. They lived close together down south of Dardanelle, and they were well known in the area for the mischief they created trying to make a quick buck without doing any actual work. Their latest escapade was letting themselves be hired to break into a gas line that ran across Garnet's Uncle ADD's property up north of London. Uncle ADD had just peppered their behinds with buckshot when the pipe blew, throwing them into a patch of cactus, and throwing ADD onto a muddy creek bank.

The twins were paroled early because of prison overcrowding and good behavior (go figure). Part of their parole agreement was that they find steady work. That was easier said than done given their track record, but after some local arm twisting, they found work at Bach's Funeral Service and Hazen's Livery respectively. They worked at night thus staying out of the public eye.

On the night in question, Johnny Joe was alone in the back of the Bach building. Mr. Bach himself had supervised rolling two body tables into the back near the delivery ramp. He had placed a large envelope of disposal instructions on each of the bodies. When the livery driver came, he would check the envelopes and take the bodies to their appropriate destinations. The name, Justice, was written with a Sharpie on one envelope, Summermann, on the other.

Johnny Joe hated this job. It was always cold down here in the morgue because bodies had to be kept cool to prevent decomposition. And, more to the point, Johnny was more than a little afraid of the dead bodies. He had grown up with spooky stories about ghosts and evil spirits. Sometimes he'd unzip one of the body bags and peer inside, but he never actually touched any part of a corpse.

On this particular night, Johnny had started drinking early. The night job was lonely with no one else there, so he usually brought along a little liquid medication to give him courage as he sat there thinking about the dead bodies. He had only recently discovered that the embalmer stored pure grain alcohol in the prep room. Johnny Joe was afraid to take too much at a time, but he'd take just a little now and then and replace it with water. He'd had a little last night to help him over the frustration of a flat tire when he left for work late.

He hadn't planned to have any tonight, but his wife picked up the mail and found an overdue notice for that rifle he'd bought on the sly. She had reamed him from one end to the other, and by the time he finally made it in to work, he really needed a stiff drink. So he sat there, feeling sorry for himself because of the rifle, knowing he'd have to cut back on the liquor just to pay for it. As he drank more alcohol, he became more morose and began talking to the two bodies, telling them how lucky they were that they didn't have a cheap wife like his. Then he realized he didn't know if they were even male. If they were women, they wouldn't have a wife, would they?

As he drank even more, his addled brain went round and round the conundrum of whether women ever had wives, and more importantly, whether a dead man could have a wife. He finally decided to settle his confusion by determining whether the bodies were male or female. If they were both female, then problem solved.

He was weaving just a little as he made his way over to the bodies and unlocked their wheels so that he could pull them under the big fluorescent ceiling light for better viewing. He had just unzipped the upper part of a body bag and peered in at the woman inside when a hand clamped down on his shoulder.

"What are you doing in there?" a low voice asked.

Johnny Joe was terrified. It didn't matter which haint it was, he had to get away! He screamed and flung himself forward with his arms straight out. He fell face down onto the corpse, pushing the rolling table full force into the second table which rolled into his desk. Realizing he was lying across a corpse with his face nearly inside the body bag, he backed up, screaming, "No! No! Lord help me!" Then he heard the sound of laughter that he recognized.

"You son of a bitch!," he yelled at Johnny Earl who was doubled over with laughter. "You like to have scared me to death! You got no business sneakin' in here like that!"

"If you could have seen yourself," Johnny Earl straightened up and wiped tears of laughter from his eyes. "I really had you goin' there."

"I'll have you goin' somewhere!" Johnny Joe shook a fist at his cousin.

"Now, now, I was just havin' some fun. I didn't know you'd sling them tables all over tha room." He was still laughing to himself. "What time is it?" he looked at the clock on the wall. "I got just enough time for a drink. Here let me help you straighten this mess out." He pushed the tables back into position for easy loading and picked up the envelopes with the names on them, placing them back on top of the body bags.

"Well, that explains a lot," Garnet commented flatly, knowing what the Johnny twins were capable of. "Oh well, what else do we know?"

"I talked to Clifford Bach. He has a funeral this afternoon, but can talk to one of us after 5:00. Are you game?" Dr. Garrison asked.

"Sure. I'll be heading that direction on my way home anyway. I'll be happy to talk to the man. Boy, is he in for a surprise."

Bach Brothers Funeral Services had been in Dover for over 50 years. Mr. Clifford Bach was the funeral director. He had relinquished the embalming responsibilities to his nephew, Peter Bach, who was also a certified funeral director. Early on, folks would say that the body was at the Bachs. It didn't take long for the locals to refer to the esteemed establishment as "The Box", much to the annoyance of the Bach family, especially when Harp's 10BOX opened in nearby Russellville.

Garnet had been to several visitations at the funeral home and was familiar with the layout. She parked in the back and entered through a side door. Clifford Bach's office was just down the hall. He was working on some papers, but stopped immediately when she knocked at his open door.

"Come in. Come in," he rose to greet her. "Please take a seat." The wing-back chairs were deep and comfortable. As Garnet sat down, he pulled two folders from a small organizer on his desk. "Now let me see," he continued the courtesies, "you're Dr. Daniels?" he raised his eyebrows in question. When Garnet nodded, he continued. "And you're related to ADD Daniels." Garnet nodded again. Mr. Bach smiled broadly and lost his somewhat formal tone, "How is the old rascal? Haven't seen him in some time."

Garnet smiled back. She hadn't realized that Uncle ADD could be such an ice breaker. "I'd say he's up to his usual stunts. The last time I saw him he was talking some nonsense about a moonstone." She neglected to tell him she'd seen Uncle ADD just last night, or what Uncle ADD had dug up.

"A moonstone?" he queried. "I haven't heard about anybody using a moonstone for, oh say, 30 or 40 years. Is he having any luck?" he laughed at the rhetorical nature of his question.

"I think he dug up some rotten pieces of an old bridle," she laughed too.

"Well, just as long as he doesn't dig up any dead people. We work too hard getting them into the ground for him to be out digging them up."

Garnet took a deep breath and smiled her agreement. Clifford Bach had no idea how close he was to the truth!

Mr. Bach moved back to his business persona. "I understand there has been some mix-up stemming from our livery service. What is your understanding of the problem?"

"We received the body of Ms. Ella Justice with the donated body paperwork for Ms. Summermann, minus her death certificate. Ms. Justice was a registered body donor, but we don't have any current paperwork for her, including the death certificate."

"Let me see. Let me see." Mr. Bach perused the papers inside the two folders. "This is Ms. Summermann's death certificate and paperwork which you don't need because you don't have her body. Ms. Justice's paperwork is in order, but her file is marked 'CREMATION'." He turned the file toward Garnet so she could see for herself. "Oh, dear," he spoke mostly to himself. "If you have Ms. Justice, then Ms. Summermann's body must have gone to the crematorium?" he smiled wanly.

"Yes, we think that's the most likely scenario. And it seems even more likely when you add the Johnny twins into the mix."

"Ah, yes, the Johnny twins. I shudder to think what else they've mixed up."

"I think we can clear up this unfortunate situation fairly easily," Garnet offered. "We need the death certificate for Ella Justice so that we can legally use her body. You need the body of Ms. Summermann. Since our donors agree to cremation of their bodies following use, and since it's very likely that she has already been cremated, all you have to do is find out where the ashes are now." She knew she was being somewhat cavalier since she had a pretty good idea where those ashes were.

Mr. Bach was only too happy to agree to the solution. He checked further and found that the presumed ashes of Ella Justice had been picked up by the driver for Golden Rod Acres. This was fairly routine when there were no relatives listed. Golden Rod Acres had a beautiful memorial garden where ashes could be scattered unobtrusively, and residents with relatives even asked occasionally for their ashes to be scattered in a favorite place in the garden.

Mr. Bach promised to check with Golden Rod Acres tomorrow to confirm the location of the ashes, and Garnet said her polite good byes and headed for home.

On the way home a niggling thought bothered Garnet. Ella Justice had been with the Anatomy Department for several years, and Garnet was sure she had a niece who was in graduate school in North Carolina. Garnet needed to check Ella's records first thing tomorrow morning in case there was a relative still out there.

10

Garnet made a note to herself to check the Donated Body records for Ella Justice's file, especially now that she had the required death certificate. It would be a simple matter to call Mr. Hartman downstairs to have him pull up the file and add the death certificate. Right now she had a class waiting.

When Garnet returned from her class, there was a phone message from Mr. Bach. He had checked with Golden Rod Acres, and they had assured him that the ashes had been scattered in their memorial garden last spring. End of problem. But it wasn't the end of the problem for Garnet. She still had the box of ashes with Ella Justice's name on it on her dining table at home!

Later that afternoon as Garnet and Mr. Hartman went through Ella Justice's donated body forms, Garnet verified to herself that Ella did have a niece who was authorized to claim the ashes. She wrote down the name, address, and phone number of Dr. Scarlett Mars in North Carolina, knowing that Dr. Mars may have moved several times since the donated body forms had been filed.

Ella's death certificate seemed in order, indicating that she had died of natural causes. Garnet didn't recognize the signature of Patricia Lewis, RN. "Is it legal for a nurse to sign a death certificate?" she queried Mr. Hartman.

"Yes," he replied. "It doesn't happen often, but it is legal. We had several like that when I was in the business. If a patient dies of natural causes in a nursing home, then it's legal for the Charge Nurse to sign the death certificate.

Golden Rod Acres is not really a nursing home, but because they offer assisted living, then technically they qualify."

That night, Garnet called the North Carolina number in Raleigh, only to get a person who had never heard of Scarlett Mars. So she went to the internet and found references to Dr. Mars associated with Agriculture Departments at NCSU and Clemson. Those calls would have to wait until tomorrow.

The next day at noon, Garnet contacted the two Ag Departments, searching for Dr. Mars. The east coast states were an hour ahead so Garnet was hoping the office personnel had returned from lunch. Here at MNSU the place practically shut down at lunch. To her surprise, the departmental chair at NCSU picked up the phone.

"NCSU Ag. This is David Stratton."

"This is Dr. Garnet Daniels from Mount Nebo State University in Arkansas. I'm trying to locate Dr. Scarlett Mars because of a death in the family."

"I am (he drawled it out as one word) sorry to hear that. But no, Scarlett isn't here anymore. She took a postdoc at Clemson to study muscadines. She should be gone by now, but they can probably tell you where she is."

The next call was more fruitful, so to speak. The secretary transferred her to the department chair, August Stein. Garnet repeated her story.

"Ah, yes, Dr. Scarlett. An impressive young lady. Not too good with the statistics, but a good researcher. She's been working on muscadines. I fully expect her to develop a new variety. Probably call it the Scarlett Muscadine," he laughed. "She's not here."

"Do you know where she is?" Garnet kept fishing.

"Oh yes, sorry" he paused. "She went to UC Davis for the summer, working with the Muscadine Consortium. (They have tons of money.)" He gave her the number for the Ag Department there.

Garnet was beginning to feel as if she were on a merry-go-round. California was two hours behind central time, so she'd wait to call just before she went home. When she made her late afternoon call, she reached the Program Director for fruit research. She asked about Dr. Mars.

"She's not here." *Why does that not surprise me?* "You missed her by two weeks. We'd love to have her here; she's a good fruit scientist, and she helped us quite a bit with our muscadines. That new variety she's working on should make a fine wine."

"Do you know where she is now?" Garnet asked hopefully.

"Why sure, she's back in your neck of the woods. She's Assistant Professor for Research at the University of Arkansas." He gave her the number for the Ag Department's fruit research lab at the UofA and a cell number that might or might not be current.

It was after 5:00, but Garnet knew that researchers didn't keep a strict clock, so she dialed the number. And who should pick up but the ever moving Dr. Scarlett Mars herself!

"Dr. Mars?" Garnet couldn't believe her luck. "This is Dr. Garnet Daniels from the Anatomy Department at MNSU, and..."

"Oh yes," Dr. Mars interrupted, "my Aunt Ella mentioned you when she worked there."

"Well, it's your Aunt Ella I wanted to talk to you about. We have some questions about her donated body forms," Garnet hedged the subject.

"Oh, well you can ask her. She's out at Golden Rod Acres in assisted living. Her body is failing, but her mind's still sharp, or it was when I talked to her in March."

Garnet was dumbfounded. Something was really wrong. Scarlett should have been notified.

"You said donated body. Is there something I need to know?" Scarlett caught on quickly.

The silence at Garnet's end of the conversation spoke volumes. She gathered her thoughts then continued. "I'm sorry to be the one to tell you. But Ella died in March. There's been some mix up at the funeral home, and Mr. Bach thought she had been cremated, even though we have her body."

Scarlett paused briefly before uttering, "Shit!" Then she continued, "I knew she wasn't answering her phone. I was going to come down there, but I just got moved here, and... Oh well, I screwed the pooch on that one. What can I say?"

"Would it be possible for you to make a trip down here soon?" Garnet inquired. "We do have her body, if you want to see her. And, we have lots of questions about why you weren't informed. I plan to make a quick trip out to Golden Rod Acres tomorrow to try to tie up some loose ends. Maybe I'll learn something there."

"I'd really appreciate that," Scarlett sounded relieved. I can't make it down until Friday evening, if that's all right with you."

"Yes, that'll be fine. Come for dinner. You're welcome to spend the night with us. We have a nice guest room waiting. By the way, do you have a copy of her will?"

Scarlett sighed, "yes somewhere in all that stuff in my apartment. I'll dig it out before I come."

They exchanged cell phone numbers, and Garnet gave Scarlett directions to her house.

11

Garnet hated taking work home with her, but it had to be done. She'd already spent unscheduled time by going to the Bach Brothers. Now she was shaving off some afternoon time to go out to Golden Rod Acres.

Golden Rod Acres was a small retirement village built about four years ago between Dover and the Augsburg community. It had 25 small rental garden-apartments designed for retirees of modest to middle income and a half dozen small, two-bedroom houses. All the buildings were painted a soft gold with white trim. The large main building was an Assisted Care Facility that could house up to 24 residents. The small, one-bedroom apartments for assisted living were built along glass-lined, rain-proof, corridors that joined a large central area. This area housed the administrative offices and the reception area plus several multipurpose rooms partitioned by folding doors. There was an exercise room and a TV room toward the back, and the front housed a large dining area that could be used for bingo and board games. There was also a pleasant lounge area with an upright piano. Decorations were tastefully done in golds, yellows, peaches and greens so that the large central area seemed light and cheery.

When Garnet approached the reception desk, a woman with a volunteer tag looked at her and smiled, inviting questions. Not sure that the mix-up was entirely the fault of the Johnny twins, Garnet decided to play the role of sleuth. She smiled broadly at the woman and stated her mission, "I'm here to see Ella Justice. Would you give me her apartment number?"

The smile on the woman's face froze, and she hesitated before turning her chair to the far side of her desk. "I'm afraid you'll need to talk to Nurse Hannah about that. I'll get her for you." She darted out of the reception cubicle down the hall toward the administrative offices, entered an open door, and pulled it shut. Almost immediately a short, plump woman in scrubs came through the door and hurried toward Garnet.

"Hello, I'm Hannah Gibson, nursing supervisor." She smiled and offered her hand. "You were inquiring about Ella Justice"

"Yes, I haven't heard from her for a while, so I thought I'd come by for a visit," Garnet repeated her mission while noticing that neither woman had asked for her name.

Nurse Hannah's face became somber. "I'm afraid Ms. Justice died here in March. I believe her death certificate said 'natural causes'".

"I knew she was in Assisted Living, but I had no idea she was that sick," Garnet appeared to be genuinely surprised.

"Oh, yes, she was getting weaker and weaker, and that last week, she was practically non-responsive. We were making plans to move her to a nursing home. We don't offer skilled nursing here. But then she died in the night."

"Were you here?" Garnet was gathering more information.

"No, I do some of the nursing, and all the paperwork during the day. Then I have very competent staff who take over at night. But actually, I had taken spring break to go with my daughter to Miami."

Garnet covered her mouth and closed her eyes, signaling her slow acceptance of the death. "Well, do you know where she was buried?" once again she was fishing for information.

"Oh, no, she wasn't buried. She had no next of kin listed on her records, and as far as I know, she didn't even have a will. When that happens, the deceased are cremated, and the ashes are spread in our memorial gardens. Perhaps you'd like to make a stop there before you leave?"

"Yes, I think I will." She accepted a map from the receptionist and was turning to leave when she heard the piano start up. "Is that Maynard?" she asked, smiling again.

"You mean Ms. Tanner, don't you?" Nurse Hannah's voice was disapproving now.

"Oh, I never knew her last name, or her first name for that matter. I just knew her sister who told me Maynard was living here, and that she loved to play the piano."

"Well, her name is Mabel Tanner. And I'll leave it to her sister to explain how she got that ridiculous name!" Nurse Hannah turned on her heel and marched off toward her office.

Garnet thanked the volunteer for her help and turned her face toward the front door. She detoured toward the piano sound and watched as a little woman in a blue flowered shirt and blue pants played enthusiastically while the gathering crowd sang along, happily clapping, some in unison, some not.

When Maynard paused between requests, Garnet approached the piano and introduced herself. "I'm Garnet Daniels. Your sister Ethyl mentioned you several times at Summer Book Club. She said to look you up if I ever got out this way."

"Oh, yes," Maynard smiled brightly. "You're the college professor Ethyl told me about. She said you really added to the entertainment value. Those women are a hoot. I don't know when they ever get around to talkin' about their books."

"I was just out here to ask about an old friend (maybe you knew her), Ella Justice. I hate to admit it, but I didn't realize that she had passed."

"Oh, yes, I know all about her," Maynard said mysteriously.

"Is there something I should know?" Garnet took the bait.

"Maybe. Maybe not," Maynard was deliberately being secretive. "Maybe you could come back this weekend, and we could talk."

Garnet suspected she was being gamed by a lonesome little lady who didn't have many visitors. People tended to forget friends in retirement villages. They had so many planned activities, how could they get lonely? Oh well, what the heck? "How about Sunday afternoon, say 2:00 or 3:00?"

Maynard smiled broadly. That would be just fine. I'll have time to bake a little somethin' special. She gave Garnet her apartment number and pointed in the direction out west of the main building toward the pond.

As Garnet looked up when she turned to go, she saw Nurse Hannah looking squarely at her, and she was not smiling. In fact her body language was almost hostile. Maybe there was something here after all.

The map of the complex showed four rows of duplexes separated by two single car garages, a recreation area with badminton and tennis courts, a horseshoe pitching area, and a disc-golf course. There was a big pond where fishing was allowed, and walking trails followed the lengthy outside perimeter. Up in the northeast corner, an area had been set aside for contemplation, and the memorial gardens were immediately adjacent.

As Garnet turned toward the memorial gardens, she passed the administrative wing. There again was Nurse Hannah, watching her through her office window. Although the surveillance was irritating because of its pettiness, Garnet chalked it up to alpha female syndrome. The alpha female needed to keep control in her own domain. The presence of another alpha female (Garnet) could be mildly threatening.

Garnet walked up the gently sloped hill to the gardens which were beautifully landscaped, and truly peaceful. Maybe Ella could come here after all, when she was finally cremated.

12

Hannah was relieved when she saw Garnet head toward the parking lot. She hadn't expected anyone to ask about Ella Justice, and Garnet's visit had thrown her off. Oh well, she had handled the situation, even if a little frostily. She hated to admit that she was uncomfortable with the Ella Justice situation. Surprisingly, Ella had died while Hannah was on vacation. She had seemed fine when Hannah left. But Rose Cassidy, the director of Golden Rod Acres had assured Hannah that Ella had gone down so fast that everyone was surprised. Still, there might have been some medical intervention that could have been attempted.

Just for reassurance, she used her burner phone to call her old mentor, Dimitri Popolov, in Florida. They had been lovers briefly when Marcia had bailed on her. When the small fire died, their business sense took over, and he had trained her to be an account manager in one of his numerous small businesses. She still called him from time to time when she felt down.

Dimitri actually answered the phone. She had expected to be playing phone tag with him as usual. "Hey, Babe," his raspy voice greeted her, "are you still building on your house?" Building a house was code for hiding money, supposedly for the future. "How's Randi (Miranda) doing over there in Indian Territory? Is she a Cherokee yet?"

"No. But she's trying her best. She's dating a guy who's a member of the Cherokee Nation, but I don't think that's going to do it."

"Gotta go," he ended the call abruptly. She figured he had a hot prospect on another line.

Miranda, Miranda, Miranda, just two more years and God knows where you'll be, she thought to herself. She didn't know what the chances were that she could hold her daughter, her poor motherless daughter.

It was 22 years now. In some ways it seemed like 100, and in others it seemed like yesterday. Hannah Gibson and Marcia Torres had fallen madly in love. Marriage wasn't legal for them then in Florida, but they had a small ceremony and pledged their undying love. After about a year, they decided they needed a child to complete their family.

Hannah didn't particularly want or even need a child. But Marcia was driven to become a mother. A child. A child. They simply must have a child. Finally they opted for artificial insemination. It took them a while to find a clinic that would help them, once the personnel learned that they were two lesbians planning to raise a child. Quite a few people disapproved of that arrangement, and it was even illegal in some states.

They hadn't put any caveats on the father, knowing that donors at their clinic had to pass a comprehensive battery of physical and psychological tests before being accepted. Nevertheless, they were somewhat taken aback when the baby came. She had dark hair and skin and almost black eyes. Her cheek bones were high. And there she was: their little papoose!

Marcia was ambivalent about the baby from the beginning, but she decided to give motherhood the old college try. They named the baby Miranda, and Marcia basked in all the attention that her beautiful new offspring brought. People would stop in the grocery store or the street to talk baby talk to the happy, smiling baby. Yet Marcia held back from full commitment, unable to shake her own prejudice against things Native American.

The agreement between the two mothers was that Hannah would work and Marcia would be the stay-at-home mom. Marcia was alternately happy with her lot then cool toward Hannah who was not tied to the apartment and the child. Hannah tried very hard to be understanding. She worked three twelve-hour shifts in the ER at a local hospital so she could be home with her family. When she was home, Marcia went "out" most of the time, going to her Zumba class, volunteering at a thrift shop, meeting with a group of writers, etc. She even insisted on doing the grocery shopping by herself to get more personal time.

Hannah thought Marcia would be relieved when Miranda started preschool two days a week, but Marcia complained that the routine of dropping Miranda off, then retrieving her three hours later was chopping up her day and making it impossible for her to get anything done. It was increasingly clear that Marcia resented Miranda and the changes in life style her presence required.

Then one day someone from Miranda's school called to inform Hannah that Miranda had not been picked up after morning preschool. Hannah arranged to trade part of her shift with another nurse and hurried to the school, fully expecting to find her daughter scared and in tears. Not so. Miranda was settled in an alcove outside the main office watching a video of the Three Little Pigs, learning to count. "Hi, Mom," she looked up at Hannah, "there are three little pigs and one big bad wolf. That makes four."

The "Dear Hannah" letter was on the counter under the coffee pot. Marcia had taken all of her own things and quite a few of Hanna's. She was not coming back. Hannah cried her eyes out and blamed herself for not loving Marcia enough to overcome any rough patches in their marriage. Yet, at some level she was relieved. The constant complaining about how unfair life was and the persistent coolness to Mirada had become an emotional burden.

Hannah's life changed during the next two weeks. She changed to day shifts so she could be home with Miranda every night. She was lucky to find a reputable day-care near school that would pick up Miranda and several of her class mates every day and watch them until evening. Hannah used the money she saved from supporting Marcia to cover the bills and even saved a little. It was her day shift activities that opened another door for Hannah.

Hannah was surprised to find that she was actually happier without Marcia. Still, she went into a mild depression, feeling overwhelmed by all the responsibilities she shouldered alone now. To make matters worse, a mutual friend informed her Marcia was dating again, this time, a man! *That tears it!* Marcia thought to herself. *No wonder she was in such a hurry to dump me. But Miranda?*

How could she just walk off and leave her? Marcia's name is on the birth certificate. I have no legal standing. What am I going to do?

Fortunately (for her) Hannah had nursed a lawyer with peritonitis from a ruptured appendix, reassuring him that it truly did get better later. He had told her to call him if she needed legal advice, so she did. He referred her to Child Protective Services. Hannah didn't want to be approved as a foster parent. She wanted to have a legal tie to Miranda. She wanted to raise her as her own! With her lawyer's help, she got the court to appoint her as Miranda's guardian. Now she could plan for Miranda's future without fear of legal repercussions, and she could even take her out of state. Good deal!

Miranda became better adjusted at school. Hannah had feared that her child would be teased for her Seminole-like features. Instead the kids had immediately jumped on the fact that Miranda had two mothers and no father. They were relentless in their claims that the entire family was going to Hell. Then when Marcia left and there was only one mother, the harassment stopped. It wasn't at all unusual for a child to be living with a single parent.

13

Hannah was in the cardiac ICU when she met Dimitri. He had undergone open heart surgery and was not doing well. It was as if he never had come completely out from under the anesthetic. His doctor diagnosed him with Post-perfusion Syndrome, also known as "Pump Head". The disability was characterized by confusion and loss of cognitive function (inability to read and comprehend, or to complete simple crossword puzzles or basic arithmetic problems). Often the gait was irregular, and vertigo could be pronounced. The disorder usually resolved within two months, although it could last as long as five years.

Dimitri was aware enough to know that he needed some serious assistance, so he offered Hannah a job as his home-care nurse. She turned him down gently, explaining that she had a six-year-old at home. Then he sweetened the pot. She could bring her daughter with her. He had plenty of room. And his driver would take Miranda to school and pick her up in the afternoon. Hannah would have no living expenses, and the salary was twice what she was making now. She could start a college fund for Miranda.

Hannah couldn't believe her eyes when she saw the house. It was more like a palace. There were halls and rooms everywhere, not to mention servants' quarters. Only one person, the housekeeper, stayed there during the week while the chef, driver, gardener, and any number of others came in and out. Hannah and Miranda were given a suite on the first floor to which Dimitri had been relocated. Climbing stairs was out of the question for him.

The first month was challenging. Dimitri kept pretending nothing was wrong. But Hannah could easily tell that something was. He was healing nicely from the surgery, but the "Pump Head" symptoms had him terrified inside. He failed to tell her that his vision was blurry. Whenever she handed him anything to read, he suddenly needed to nap. She brought him a large-print book of crosswords which he pretended to appeciate. Then she saw him fling it across the room in frustration when his vision, dexterity, and memory colluded to foil him.

The trips to various specialists seemed endless. Not only was there the cardiologist, but also the ophthalmologist, the neurologist, the physical therapist, and the psychologist. Dimitri believed that if he could just get the right medication, everything would be back to normal within a few days. But each specialist he visited told him what he needed was time, not another batch of pills.

Early in the second month, he began to improve. His progress was amazing. By the end of the month, he could get up from his chair without staggering across the floor to catch his balance. He could use the toilet without help getting up and down. He could shower himself without fear of falling. And, although it took him two afternoons, he worked one of the large-print crossword puzzles.

Considering his progress, and the amount of help he already had available to him, Hannah assumed he was ready for her to leave. But he talked her into staying another month, just in case. Miranda was thrilled. She and Dimitri had bonded. Now he was her best adult friend and sometimes playmate. She called him Uncle Pop-Pop, and he called her Randi-Pop.

The relationship lasted six years. Hannah had a good head for business, and Dimitri made her the manager at his scrubs store. Her good eye for color and fashion and her easy way of communicating with medical personnel gave the store a good reputation, and the profits started increasing after the first month.

Dimitri was quite the entrepreneur. He had ten small businesses in the area and substantial rental property. But it didn't take long for Hannah to figure out that something was wrong. There were lots of people, both male and female, coming and going at all hours. They all carried small, fat zippered bank deposit pouches. Dimitri would usher them into his office, and soon they would leave with a flatter pouch or even a completely different pouch. He had a web business buying and selling antique office equipment requiring couriers to move the goods around. *Why do you need a courier for an antique fountain pen?*

14

The rest of Garnet's week was filled with the usual lectures and labs. The students were now working on the lower extremity where the muscles were large and easy to identify. Students were amazed to find that major blood vessels left the body on the anterior (front) side of the body, but ended up on the posterior (back) side of the leg via the *adductor hiatus*, an opening in the muscles near the knee. Thus the rule that blood vessels and nerves cross on the flexor (bending) side of the joints was maintained. Most people knew where their quads and hams were located, but Garnet was always surprised that very few recognized that a pork ham at the grocery was a pig's thigh.

Garnet checked on the legal status of cremains and determined that she could keep Uncle ADD's boxes for the time being. They would likely be added to the set of boxes from the anatomy lab that would be interred at a special ceremony next spring. Cremains were returned to family members if requested, but quite a few were unclaimed.

Thursday was ladies' lunch day. Professional women from the State Crime Lab located at Mt. Nebo State University (MNSU) and Detective Seargent Sophia Calypso from the Dardanelle Police Department, plus Garnet and a few others from time to time met regularly to talk and vent over lunch. This Thursday, Dr. Rachel Pachebelle, State Medical Examiner, was present, and Garnet couldn't wait to pull her aside to ask her about the events surrounding Ella Justice's mysterious death, pseudo-cremation, and appearance at the Anatomy Department's morgue. Rachel assured her that, considering the

Johnny twins role in the mix-up, there was probably nothing to worry about. The real puzzler was how the bag of cremains got into the center of that burial plot.

Garnet was looking forward to meeting Dr. Scarlett Mars. She wondered if she would have flowing black hair like that other Scarlett in *Gone With the Wind*. Scarlett had light brown hair highlighted with gold and reddish bands that gave her a warm look. She was large framed and big boned, and her athletic look gave her a sense of physical competence.

When Scarlett arrived at the house, Garnet asked if she wanted to bring an overnight bag in. "No," Scarlett declined. "Thank you, but I have to be in the field tomorrow morning at 6:30, so I'd better get back up the road tonight. I can get more sleep that way."

Garnet introduced her husband, Mica, an economics professor, and poured beer mugs of iced tea. Scarlett and Mica both added two packets of sweetener, southern style, but Garnet drank hers straight. As they sipped their tea, Scarlett filled them in on her relationship with her now dead aunt.

Scarlett's mother, Anna, and Ella were estranged (Scarlett wasn't sure what the row had been about. Both women clammed up grimly when prodded for information), but Scarlett had managed to keep some contact with Ella, who had no children. Hence she was the beneficiary of Ella's will. Scarlett had found her copy of the will which she laid out on the table. She also had a lock box key, and Ella had told her to open it if something happened to her. Scarlett had been to the box with Ella, and she was pretty sure the box contained another copy of the will, Ella's passport, and some heirloom jewelry, including the elk's tooth.

When Garnet asked, Scarlett described the tooth. Grandfather Garner had joined the Fraternal Order of Elks in the late 1950s. As part of the initiation, he was presented with a real elk's tooth with a gold cap studded with semiprecious stones. Scarlett remembered the shiny red, blue, yellow and green gems around the edge of the finding. The tooth had a small gold chain that was pinned into a pocket so that the little treasure hung out over the edge. Scarlett remembered coveting the little tooth with its tiny stones as a girl.

Mica had made an excellent dish of chicken parmesan and a big Caesar salad with cheesecake for dessert. The three chatted about Scarlett's work while they ate, and Mica was intrigued by the statistical methods that were required to sort varieties of grapes. Then there were the gene linkages that had to be documented. Before long, he was offering to help with any statistical analysis Scarlett might need in the future. Statistics was one of Mica's great loves.

After dinner, Scarlett spread the pages of the will out on the table for perusal. Ella had left small gifts of money to several nieces and nephews and a larger sum to the Arkansas Children's Hospital. And as already known, she had willed her body to the medical school. The remainder of the estate went to Scarlett.

"Do you have signature rights on any of Ella's accounts?" Garnet asked.

"No, I'm just the beneficiary. The lock box is the only thing I have access to as of today."

"I see," said Garnet who had some knowledge of wills. "There's a good chance that the will is going to have to be probated. Do you know who her attorney is?"

"Yes. He's one of her old friends. And he'll be the executor of the will. I've met him a couple of times. I'll get in touch with him Monday. Do you know of any thing I can do right away?"

"Well, you can go ahead and get death certificates that will be required to freeze her accounts, although her bank accounts have probably been frozen since last March when she died. You'll need to go to the Bach Brothers Funeral Services in Dover to get copies of the certificate. Do you know what other accounts she had? She would have had Social Security and State retirement, plus who knows what."

Scarlett shook her head no. "I just hope her lawyer has all of that. It might be in the lockbox." Her expression indicated that she was beginning to see how complicated things could become.

"Then, I'd get about ten notarized copies of the death certificate. They'll be needed for all her accounts before the will can be probated."

"All right," Scarlett was resigned, "I should be able to get back down here on Monday to meet the lawyer and to get the ball rolling. I'll go by the bank and get everything out of her lockbox. There may be something in there that will help."

15

Garnet had Saturday off. Usually she prepared a lunch to share with Uncle ADD and Beulah when they returned from Sabbath services at Dardanelle. Uncle ADD considered himself to be a Spiritual Jew, and he had joined a Messianic Christian group that met weekly in Dardanelle. This week ADD and Beulah were skipping Saturday services since they planned to participate in the March of Remembrance on Sunday. Christian, Jewish, and Messianic leaders and interested people marched together biannually in remembrance of the Holocaust and in support of Israel.

Minus Uncle ADD, Garnet had time to catch up on paper work, plan the coming week's lectures, and even watch a TV program. Sunday, she had promised to visit Maynard out at the retirement home.

The late August afternoon was hot and dry. The region badly needed rain to break the mini-drought, but rain was not coming today. The grasses and weeds along the highway showed only the palest green on a few stalks. Most were already browned and getting browner. A thin film of dust from decaying plants was everywhere, and Garnet promised herself an extra antihistamine before bedtime.

Maynard's apartment was on the east end of a row of six. A tiny dining area held a table and two chairs nestled beside the similarly tiny bay window on that side. Far from being pastoral, the view was of the assisted living center, and Garnet noticed a pair of binoculars on the sill behind a curtain. The small living room was located on the south side, and just now there was plenty of light coming in through the double window even though the shades were drawn against the afternoon sun. There were two bedrooms down a short hall that ended in the shared bathroom between the rooms. The kitchen and an alcove with sliding doors to hide the washer and dryer adjoined the living room, and a door opened into the one-car garage. There were no windows on the north side, and with two one-car garages between Maynard and her neighbor on the west, the apartment was insulated from the northwest winds of winter.

Maynard was clearly excited about the visit. She ushered Garnet in and served her a tall glass of iced tea. They sat in the living room, and Garnet complimented Maynard on her décor.

"Well, I've been here four years, since the first. And I'm the only one who's lived in this apartment. I've changed quite a few things over the years, but I'm slowin' down. Your priorities change as you get older."

"How did you manage to get first dibs on this apartment?" Garnet was curious.

"Oh, my ex was workin' for the Housing Authority. And we don't always get along (that's why he's my ex), but he knew I was lookin', and he got my name in early. There were only three names ahead of me, and they didn't want to be this close to the assisted care building. So..."

"Being this close to assisted care doesn't bother you?"

"No. I really wanted that little dining room with the bay window. I always wanted one of those little bay window thingies like the rich folks have, and I figured this was as close as I'd ever get. Besides, since I moved in, my ex, George Tanner, had a stroke and got moved into assisted care. Now I can keep an eye on him. Make sure he's gettin' good care."

Garnet remembered the binoculars in the window. Maynard might literally be keeping an eye on George. "Is the care here good?" she was hoping for an honest evaluation.

Maynard hesitated just a tad before replying. "Yeah, for the most part. You have to be able to walk, and you have to be able to feed yourself, so it's not like bein' in a nursing' home. But it seems to me they're awfully quick to send you off to a nursin' home if you have any little downturn. If they'd wait a week or so, some folks would pull out of it."

"But they told me Ella Justice went down so fast that she died before they could get her transferred. Do very many people actually die out here?" Garnet was fishing.

"Well, no, not many. Only two or three. They all start gettin' dizzy, and kind of confused. Then pop! Before you know it they're gone."

"What do their families say?"

"I don't reckon there's much they can say. Dead is dead. It's funny how the families run. Some folks out here have more relatives than ants on a hill, and they all come on Sunday afternoon and try to squeeze into that little cubby hole, especially if their 'loved one' has some money to leave. Then there's others that don't have a big family here in the valley, and they spend their Sundays out in the Rec room. I'll go over after a while and play for them."

"What about those who don't have anyone?"

"I feel real sorry for them. They're usually the first to go. I just don't think it's good for a body to be all alone, even if it's your own fault. There's some folks that are so mean to their families, it's no wonder they don't get anyone comin' to see them!"

Garnet decided to change the topic so her prying wouldn't be so obvious. "Do you ever fish in that big pond?" she motioned toward the west.

"Yeah, I go over there a lot when it's not so dad-blamed hot. I take me a foldin' chair and a cooler and lots of mosquito spray. As dry as it is, they still seem to find me. I think I'm just too sweet smellin' for them."

"I know what you mean," Garnet sympathized. I have a good friend who swears by Avon's Skin So Soft, but it doesn't do anything for me. I need Deep Woods Deet.

"Speakin' of something' sweet smellin', I made us a little treat," Maynard headed for the tiny kitchen. "You just sit there, and I'll bring it out. Do you need more tea?"

Garnet shook her head, and soon Maynard came back with two plates of a pale yellow pie with piles of meringue.

"Mmm, that looks good. I love a good meringue," Garnet offered.

"I don't know if you've ever had this. It's vinegar pie. It was my mother's favorite from the depression when they didn't have fresh lemons," Maynard explained. "It sounds weird, but it's really pretty good." She sat down and watched expectantly for Garnet to take a bite.

Garnet couldn't believe how good it was. She wouldn't have to lie at all.

"Oh, my," she smiled at Maynard. "is that good or what? I need the recipe for this."

Maynard relaxed and dug in to her own piece. "I'll get that for you the next time you come. If you'll come just a little later, you can go with me over to the Rec room and meet some of the folks. I know they'd like that."

"Now you have to tell me where you got the name, Maynard. That's not what they called you at the reception desk." Garnet was genuinely curious.

Maynard had probably given the explanation hundreds of times, but was always ready to tell the story. "When my daughter was little, she got to that phase of callin' her parents by their first names. She couldn't talk too plain so the names got messed up a bit. She would never say Tanner; she just said Ner. Her name is Arlene. Well, she couldn't pronounce her 'rs', so she called herself Lenener. She called George Joner; and she called me Mayner. She learned to say the other names, but she always called me Mayner, which got changed to Maynard sometime before she started school."

"I understand completely," Garnet added her story. "I had an Uncle Fod. The Fod came from his brother's trying to say Phillips, which came out Fodups."

Garnet finished her pie then said her goodbyes. She made a date for two weeks later. By then, she hoped she would know more about why the people in assisted living had thought that Ella had no family.

16

Late Sunday evening, Nurse Hannah was having her weekly phone chat with her daughter, Randi (Miranda). "Hi, Hon. Didn't know what time you'd get back tonight. Did you run like the dickens?"

"Sure did, Mom. I came in third behind Sally and an MNSU girl. Man is she fast! But we had enough points overall to win the meet!"

"Well good for you! When are you coming home? Do you want to do something for Labor Day?"

"Uh, Mom, that's not going to work after all. Because we won this meet, we qualify for the Cotton Blossom Invitational next weekend. I'll be sweltering down in south Arkansas. Why don't you drive down? I'll send you the schedule."

"Well, I may do just that," Hannah replied, trying to keep the disappointment out of her voice. I imagine I'll have to fill in here. I try to let as many off as possible. It's a big deal here."

They chatted some more, and Hannah asked about fall break, knowing it was a nonstarter. There'd be another meet by then. Oh well, Randi was old enough to be on her own. They'd talk again next week.

When Randi was 12, Hannah had moved her from Demitri's protective nest. Randi was maturing physically. She was developing a nice little figure, and she had started having her periods. Hannah saw the lascivious looks some of Demitri's associates were giving the young girl. With so many people in the house at all hours, Hannah was not comfortable living there anymore.

She couldn't very well watch Randi 24 hours a day, but she felt queasy when Randi was alone in the house. Besides, it was clear to Hannah that Dimitri was involved in illegal business deals, including money laundering.

So Hannah became Nurse Hannah again. She worked in the ER for six months to renew her credentials then headed out to Eldorado, Arkansas, where Murphy Oil money was rebuilding the town.

Hannah and Randi stayed in Eldorado four years. All the time, Randi talked about going back to Florida for college. She had her heart set on becoming a Seminole at Florida State University. Eldorado had a track team, and Randi went out for cross country, mostly to enhance her image of herself as a swift Indian maiden. She was thin and athletic and a really good runner. In junior high, she worked herself up from gasping across the finish line to third on the team. She was sure the Seminoles would want her to run for them.

Hannah applied for the Director of Nursing position at Golden Rod Acres on a whim. The regional management team had a good reputation for running similar retirement villages, and the benefits were outstanding. Her time at the clothing store was considered to be a plus since it gave her management skills. When she broached the idea of moving to the Russellville/ Dover area to Randi, the response was ambivalent. Randi would be farther away from her beloved Seminoles in Florida, but there were Seminoles in Oklahoma, weren't there? At 16, she figured she'd have a better opportunity to find a strong Seminole brave in Russellville than in Eldorado.

The move to Russellville was a success. Randi fit in well with the kids with single mothers, and she ran, and usually won, the longer distance races in track. And, as she had before, she worked her way up to third in cross country. Hannah, for her part, was well suited for managing the nursing staff. She had learned years ago that keeping qualified and well trained personnel was not so easy as it looked. Her two strikes and you're out philosophy, with exceptions, caused a lot of turnover during the first six months. After that unless they had a work ethic, they usually didn't apply. The only long-term problem was the business manager, Rose Cassidy. Rose liked to skim the nursing budget from time to time (she called it borrowing) to purchase non-nursing items such as new furniture for the Rec room. Hannah kept track of every penny in her budget and could easily tell when Rose had "borrowed" from her account. Then the air got a little frosty.

Randi loved the folklore surrounding the five civilized tribes that had been removed forcibly from their eastern homes to Oklahoma. The story of suffering, death, and survival from the tyranny of the United Sates government, epitomized by President Andrew Jackson, was well documented. As Randi dug a little further into Cherokee history, she became fascinated with the chief, Sequoyah.

Sequoyah has a permanent place in Cherokee history because of his syllabary. He supposedly became fascinated by the "talking leaves" of the soldiers when he joined the army during the War of 1812. He became obsessed with creating a written form of Cherokee. He identified the sounds in his language and gave each syllable a written character. Over a period of about 10 years, he refined his system to 86 characters, then taught his daughter, A-Yo-Ka, to read the written language. Two things impressed Randi. First, Sequoyah was living in Arkansas Territory when he finished the syllabary, and second, a girl was the first one to read it!

Russellville had two elementary schools with names that reflected the history of Cherokees in Arkansas Territory. The first was Sequoyah, and the second, Dwight. The first Presbyterian mission to the Cherokees, Dwight Mission, was established on the Illinois Bayou near Russellville in 1821. Many descendants of Cephus Washburn, one of the original missionaries, are still living in the Arkansas River Valley. The site is now covered with the waters of Lake Dardanelle, but a Cherokee Crossing marker exists beside HWY-64 on the west end of the causeway.

The Washburn Park, honoring Cephus, is located on the West end of Lake Front Drive where it joins HWY-64. Lake front Drive was formerly named Dike Road. And the little park adjoining the Bona Dea trails was used extensively. Unfortunately for the city fathers, the park became a location for late night trysts between members of the gay community (as did several of the rest stations along I-40). When it was pointed out to one of the city fathers that because Dike Road was on the city map, visitors might misinterpret the name to think that lesbians were being honored in Russellville, (Not so.) it didn't take long to rename the drive to Lake Front, and a big deal was made about "cleaning up" the park which was renamed Washburn Park.

When the Cherokee agreed to leave Arkansas Territory to their enemy, the Osage, and move to Indian Territory in nearby Oklahoma in 1828, Dwight Mission followed. The mission was reestablished on Sallisaw Creek near present day Marble, Oklahoma in 1829. The old mission is used today as a Presbyterian camp and meeting facility. Sequoyah's cabin near Sallisaw, Oklahoma still stands.

Of course, Randi and her mother made several pilgrimages to both the cabin and the mission. Now that Randi was at the university in Tahlequah, Hannah would meet her in Muskogee on some weekends for lunch and shopping.

17

When Garnet came back to her office after her morning classes on Monday, there was a message to call Scarlett Mars. "Where are you?" Garnet inquired.

"I'm at Tom Wiseman's (neat name for a lawyer, isn't it). He was Aunt Ella's lawyer. And I guess he'll be mine, and boy am I going to need one!"

"Why? What's going on?"

"Well, I went to the lockbox like we talked about Friday night. But there wasn't anything there. No will. No elks tooth. Nada. Zippo!"

"Who took it? Had the rent expired?"

"I should be so lucky. Somebody forged her signature in February back about a month before she died. It couldn't have been her. If she was so sick the way everybody claims, how'd she get to the bank? I asked them if they asked for ID. They said no, not unless the signature didn't match the authorized one. And it did look pretty good."

"Oh, my," Garnet reacted. "What are you going to do now?"

"Well, I'm going to Public Safety to report the theft. Then I'll go back to the bank with one of these death certificates you had me pick up, so they can freeze all her accounts. Then I'll probably go back to Fayetteville to try to get things set up so I can come back later this week. Mr. Wiseman is the executor, so he'll have the bank print out all her accounts' activities going back to January. They can email the accounts to him, but it takes a couple of days. Maybe Wednesday, or even Thursday. Fortunately I have my copy of her will. That's how I found her lawyer. But I don't have any of her financial records.

I don't know whether she had credit cards, or special savings, or an IRA, or anything. She was going to make a list and leave it in the lockbox for me. If she did, whoever cleaned her out got all of that too."

"I can be home by 5:00," Garnet volunteered. Can you come by then so we can talk? I know a lot more people in this area than you do. I may be able to help."

"I'm going to take you up on that, but not tonight. I have to beat it back up the road to set up a new batch of samples to read tomorrow morning. Could I come later this week? I really do need to talk to someone."

OK, that will work, and it may be even better. Mica will be home Thursday and Friday night. He can probably help you with any of the financial information you pick up. Let me know what works for you."

Garnet and Mica discussed Scarlett's dilemma very late that evening after Garnet had finished her part of the big lab test in Gross Anatomy for tomorrow. She hated to admit it, but she was feeling a little disoriented. She still had the boxes of cremains from Galley Rock Cemetery with not a clue as to how they got there. She needed to begin sorting out what had really happened to Ella, and she had an anatomy course to teach. She decided to go with the course first, especially since she had some semblance of control over that. The other problems would have to wait.

The anatomy test went well for a first exam. The muscles of the lower extremity were comparatively large and easy to identify. The relationships of the arteries, nerves, veins and tendons were somewhat trickier. One of Garnet's favorite questions was about the names of the posterior (behind) leg muscles based solely on the position of the three tendons passing posterior to the *medial malleolus* of the foot. These were known as the Tom, Dick, and Harry group.

The *gluteal* (hip) muscles had been a real challenge for several of the groups during dissection. It was not unusual for American cadavers, especially female, to have four or five inches of fat between the skin and the actual underlying muscles. This situation convinced students that obesity was a real problem, and they made promises to themselves that they would always stay slim and would never, never become a "lard butt". The fat ran in rivulets as the students scraped it away with the blunt handles of their scalpels. As the tables, the tools, the gloves, and occasionally the floor became coated in slimy layers of fat, Gross Anatomy truly became gross.

The Ella problem continued Wednesday night. Scarlett was in a total panic when she called Garnet. "Hey, can I still come over tomorrow night. Mr. Wiseman called me about an hour ago. He says the accounts are really suspicious. Looks like someone has been using Aunt Ella's debit card to pull almost a thousand dollars a month out of her account since she died. And I need to talk to him tomorrow about what he says is probable identity theft. "I'm so rattled I don't know what to do!"

"Well, yes, I would expect to be a bit rattled too if it were me," Garnet soothed. I can be here by 4:00 tomorrow. Come for supper and stay as long as you need to. Your bed is still ready."

"Oh, thank you so much. I have samples to run early in the morning and a 1:00 appointment with Mr. Wiseman. Meanwhile, I'll hit the internet to find out what I need to do about identity theft. See you tomorrow evening."

18

Scarlett's eyes were red and her hair looked flat when she came to the door Thursday about 4:00. She had a carry-bag stuffed with papers so Garnet led her straight to the big dining table just outside the kitchen and poured a tall glass of tea.

"Oh, thank you. I needed that," Scarlett took a deep breath as Garnet waited with an expectant look on her face. "It's really a mess, and it really does look like identity theft. Somebody tried to withdraw funds last night not too long after they froze the account. The bank notified Mr. Wiseman this morning. The withdrawals started in January, about $300 a month. Then when she died, up to about a thousand a month."

"So what's your next step?"

"My next step is to be patient," Scarlett rolled her eyes. "I thought I was going to lose my mind last night when I pulled down information from the internet. Most sites recommended filing a report with the FTC. This is what the FTC posts on their site," she pulled a large pile of paper out of her bag and slapped it onto the table.

"You're kidding!" Garnet exclaimed.

"No, not really. But, because Aunt Ella is deceased, and because Tom Wiseman is the executer, he is going to have to track down the theft."

"Well, that's good news," Garnet responded. "You would have had a big mess on your hands with the theft occurring here, and God knows where else, and your being in Fayetteville."

Mica Manfried, Garnet's husband, came in about 5:30 carrying bar-b-qued ribs with all the sides and a container of no-sugar-added rocky road ice cream. Scarlett decided she could get used to eating with these folks.

After they cleaned up the table, Mica had Scarlett run back through the problem and what was being done to solve it. "Have you been able to do all the things suggested for stopping identity fraud?" he asked, making notes in his own mind about the process. For her part, Garnet had collected a lined yellow tablet and a mechanical pencil to start jotting down notes.

"Yes and no," Scarlett grimaced. She dug out a *New York Times* article with advice about identity theft. The first advice was to close accounts and notify credit reporting agencies. Scarlett had given Ella's bank a death certificate so that her accounts could be frozen, and Tom Weisman had requested bank statements that, unfortunately, showed someone was actively drawing funds from Ella's account. Her social security and State Retirement were still coming into her account via automatic payment, and someone was automatically taking it out. Ella's credit card was also with the bank, so it could be cancelled. But, Scarlett had no idea what other accounts her aunt might have opened through the years. That list was supposed to be in the lock box. Tom Wiseman didn't have a list either, although he did have Ella's social security number.

The second thing to do was to file an FTC report then make the information available to law enforcement and anyone else involved in investigating the theft. Mica lifted the thick stack of papers Scarlett had down loaded from the internet. "All of this?" he asked skeptically. When Scarlett nodded, he continued, "that's our government at work. They don't make things easy."

"Not only that," Scarlett complained, but it doesn't make sense in a lot of places. They have you over half-way through the form before they give you a chance to list the actual person who has experienced the theft. And, since Aunt Ella is deceased, things are really complicated, especially since we don't know about all her accounts."

"Well, Tod Wiseman is a sharp cookie," Garnet offered. "He'll know what agencies to contact, and he'll see that law enforcement is informed. He'll need their help with the investigation. Do you know whether he was planning to file your complaint with the police or the sheriff?"

"I think it'll be the sheriff. Although I made a report last week at the police department, since Aunt Ella was out of Dover city limits, that would make her case fall under the sheriff's jurisdiction."

"Yes, and I imagine the first place the sheriff's crew will start looking is Golden Rod Acres. There's something a little off out there. Which reminds me, would you be willing to come by the department tomorrow before you leave town to file a request for an autopsy? You have the right to do that as the presumptive beneficiary, and it may give us a better idea of why Ella went down so fast."

Early Friday morning the two women entered the Anatomy Department's morgue. Visitors were not allowed here without an escort. Garnet found the appropriate drawer and warned Scarlett that the body would be naked. This method prevented the condensation and therefore the mold that often appeared in a body bag.

Scarlett somberly regarded her aunt's face. "I wouldn't have recognized her," she shook her head. "She must have been really sick. But look, she still had her finger nails polished! She always liked to have her nails done. She said it was part of being dressed." She lifted one hand and stroked it gently. The cinnamon colored polish stood out in strong contrast to the ashy white skin of death.

Garnet closed the drawer and taped a DO NOT USE sign on the front in anticipation of an autopsy. Then she directed Scarlett to the State Crime Lab to fill out a request form. Scarlett's next stop would be Tom Wiseman's office where she would help him with as much information as possible for the lengthy report for the FTC and the sheriff's office.

19

Tom Wiseman worked with Scarlett to fill in as much of the information as possible on the FTC form. Then he called the FTC identity theft line and used the hand written form to give as much detail as possible. He assigned the reporting person as himself and explained as clearly as he could that he was the executor of the will for a deceased victim. His next stop was at the Pope County Sheriff's Office.

Marshall Boggs, the detective who usually handled identity thefts, was in the office and agreed to talk to Tom. Tom went through the details again, pointing out what he knew and a lot of what he didn't. He handed a copy of the hand written FTC report along with the bank statements to the detective for his perusal.

"Well, it's pretty clear that someone has the lady's debit card. Do you know if she had a credit card?"

"She had one with the bank, and it has been cancelled. I should get a print out of this year's activities either today or tomorrow."

"Any other cards or accounts?"

"We don't know, and I'm half afraid to find out. Her credit card was good for $8 thousand. And you know she could have had any number of merchants' cards. A lot of people I know carry a whole wad of specialty cards."

"Well, I'll start lookin' into it," Marshall gathered the papers into a bundle. "Give me your phone number again." He wrote it on top of the FTC forms. "I'll get this case into the hopper today if I can, but I've got some other duties to take care of. It'll probably be Monday before I can get out to Golden Rod Acres. I'll keep you informed, and you do the same." The two men shook hands, and Tom went back to his office.

True to his word, Detective Boggs headed out to Golden Rod Acres midmorning Monday. He looked at the brief directory and asked the receptionist for Ms. Rose Cassidy. The young volunteer was clearly taken aback. Detective Marshall Boggs had the distinction of being not only the lone Afro-American officer on the sheriff's force, but in all of Pope County. The curious lady led him down the hall to Rose's door where she blurted out, "there's a policeman here to see you!" as if Rose were in great danger.

Rose was surprised herself. She had heard of the sheriff's new hire, but had yet to meet him. She held out her hand cordially and introduced herself. "Now what can I do for you?" she asked pleasantly.

"I'm here about a patient who died here back in March, a Ms. Ella Justice." He had given her this meager statement so that he could watch her response.

Rose's face was sober now. "Oh, yes, Ella. That was a really sad situation. She was going down so fast, we were going to have to transfer her to a nursing home, but she died in the night."

"Were you able to notify her next of kin?"

"Why, no. We looked through all her admission papers, and her correspondence. If she had anyone, we didn't know it. It was really a sad thing."

Marshall wrote something down on the pad he carried. "Did you notify the bank?"

"Yes we did. We had already informed the bank that she would be leaving us and to cancel her automatic payment to us. The contract was good for the entire month, so we left it at that."

"Did you send them a death certificate?"

"Oh, no. We don't handle anything like that. That is supposed to come from her family or her estate."

"But you were unaware of any family?"

"None to my knowledge. I see what you're getting at. But what difference could it make if her accounts just sat there until somebody showed up? I'm guessing somebody did, or you wouldn't be here."

"Yes, Ma'am, that's correct. Marshall didn't offer any other information, much to Rose's disappointment. "Speaking of accounts, do you have records of any accounts she might have had?"

Rose nodded solemnly, "yes, I can probably help you there. We keep our patients' personal belongings for them in our safe here. You'd be surprised how many debit cards are misplaced in a month. Let me check to see if Rose had anything." She left the room to open a safe in a closed room, then returned. "Here we are," she handed him a small manila envelope. This is what she left. I'm so glad somebody finally came for it. I guess this belongs to whoever," she trailed off, "you found."

"Yes, Ma'am, that's correct," Marshal nodded his head, giving her no new information.

"Well, I'll have to inventory the contents and have you sign a receipt," she said a little too bluntly.

Marshall nodded his agreement, and opened the envelope. Inside were an Amazon card, a credit card from the bank, a Shell Oil card, A Missouri Southern University card, and a debit card. A driver's license and a voter registration card were there too. Rose listed the contents, and Marshall signed and dated the receipt, keeping a pink copy for himself.

As he stood and thanked Rose for her help, she explained to him that Golden Rod Acres cancelled all automatic bank draws when a resident left for any reason. He thanked her again and exited her office, leaving her to wonder what the hell was going on.

As he started down the hall, a door opened, and he nearly collided with an elderly gentleman exiting the office on a walker. "I am so sorry," he apologized. "I almost knocked you down."

"Nah, it takes more than that," the man said stolidly.

"Herb's a pretty tough customer," came from a woman's voice inside the office. She followed Herb out and asked, "are you sure you want to go by yourself? You know I'll be happy to walk with you." Herb waved her off and started down the hall at a fair clip. She turned to Marshall, "hello, I'm Gracie Preston. And you are?"

I'm Marshall Boggs," he extended his hand and felt a little spark when she took it. "I'm just out here to run down some details on a resident for a family member who's been away for a while."

"Yeah, that happens sometime. Most of our people have family somewhere, but they're not always easy to find. It really helps if we have contacts on our records."

He made small talk for a couple of minutes then left. The sign on her door said Geriatric Social Worker, whatever that was.

When he returned to his car, Marshall made detailed notes of his meeting with Rose. He used those notes when he called Tom Wiseman later that afternoon.

"Here's what I found out," he gave Wiseman the gist of his conversation with Rose. "I'm not seeing anything major wrong here, just a few flags. I understand stopping the automatic payments for Golden Rod Acres. That would save a lot of time later. But why not inform the bank that she had died?"

"Yeah, it seems a little odd, but she's right, it is the holders of the estate who usually inform and freeze all the accounts," Wiseman reasoned. "How about photocopying all those Card and faxing them to me for my records?"

Just as the fax was coming in, Tom Received a call form Mica, Garnet's husband. "Hi, Tom," Mica greeted an old acquaintance. "I'm not trying to micromanage you, little econ joke, but I've been looking at those bank printouts that Scarlett brought over. Ella Justice was getting social security and Arkansas State Retirement. Then there's a quarterly deposit from a Mutual Trust. Aside from the monthly withdrawal for Golden Rod Acres, there's a regular check for her credit card, and, one to Amazon, must be a card there. And, there's a regular check to what must be a second credit card because it has a four-digit number on the note line. Have you been able to trace any of her accounts?"

"Yes, and magically they appear! Just kidding. Marshall Boggs went out to Golden Rod Acres this morning and talked to the business manager. They had her cards locked up for her in their vault, just waiting for someone to claim them. He just faxed a copy over. Looks like there's one missing. It's that second credit card."

"Tell me again when she died," Mica was shuffling papers on his end of the line.

"March 26."

"Oh crap, someone has been writing checks on her account since then.

Here, let me see," more paper shuffling. "Damn, these signatures on the photocopies look just like hers. These are good forgeries, that's for sure. Probably the same person who cleaned out her lock box."

"What about January and February?" Tom asked.

"They look the same to me. This could have been going on for a long time. Can you get me last year's transactions too? I'll put on my forensic accountant cap and see what I can come up with."

20

Rachel Pachebelle, Medical Examiner at the State Crime Lab branch in Dardanelle, called Garnet Monday evening. "Hey, Kid, what's this autopsy request for Ella Justice about?"

Garnet had already told her friends about the mix up that had brought Ella's body to the Anatomy Department, and the mystery of why she had been headed for cremation. Now she added the theft from her lock box and the ongoing usage of her banking account.

"So," Garnet continued. "I just thought there was something fishy about the natural causes on her death certificate, and I encouraged her niece to ask for an autopsy."

"That's fair enough," Rachel responded. "I'll put suspicious death associated with demonstrated identify theft on my forms. You know the Crime Lab has to have a reason for an autopsy. I couldn't do it just because I knew Ella personally."

"Thanks, Rachel. When we first discovered her body in our morgue, we had no idea about a suspicious death. It just seemed as if the Johnny twins had been at it again. So there was no reason to request an autopsy."

"Right-oh. Now I see. I'll try to get it done this week. I'm backed up as usual, but I should be able to get to it Thursday or Friday."

By Wednesday afternoon, Tom Wiseman had a copy of Ella's bank account from last year as well as this month's bills from the bank card and Amazon. The bills were enough to make him raise his eyebrows, and he called Mica right away. "Just wait 'til you see these things. How soon can you come by? I'll make copies for you, of course."

When Mica arrived around 5:30, the two of them sat down together to look at the account information. Ella Justice had been buying some expensive merchandise since March. Prior to March, Ella's credit card payments were relatively small, and she kept a monthly balance of around $300. Now, both cards were close to the max, and the statement credited minimal payments last cycle. With minimum payments, it would take six years to pay off those two cards!

The debit card withdrawals that had been about $300 a month before Ella's death had jumped to $600 per week since March. There were some small checks to charities, but the bulk of the funds provided by deposits that had all continued since her death were written out each month to what had been assumed to be the missing credit card! Totals from the maxed credit cards, the cash withdrawals and the giant credit card payment were over $50 thousand. Someone had been bleeding Ella's account of nearly $10 thousand a month!

Garnet had just made it home late Friday afternoon when Rachel called. "Hey, Girl, what's up?" she asked when she answered the phone. "What's happening in your world?" Rachel usually had an interesting case on her hands.

"Oh my, where to start," Rachel answered. "It's been a two beer day, that's for sure. I need to talk to you about Ella's autopsy. Is it all right if I come over?"

Uh oh, Garnet thought, *she's found something serious.* "Sure, come on over. Want to stay for potluck? Mica will bring something later. I have no idea what it'll be tonight."

"Thank you, but no thanks. John and I have a date-night tonight. We get them so seldom, I don't want to miss one. I'll be there in about a half an hour."

When Rachel arrived, she carried a folder with her that she sat on the big table. Garnet could hardly wait. "What did you find?" she burst out.

"Several things I didn't want to find." Rachel answered, taking out some photos. "Do you know what these are?" she asked, showing Garnet photos of Ella's hands with the polish removed from several fingers. Garnet could see small wavy white lines across the nails.

Garnet thought a few seconds then expressed her exasperation," rats! It's back in there somewhere, but I can't call it back. Those lines are associated with some type of poisoning, but I can't remember what they're called or what the poison is."

"They're Mee's lines, and the poison is arsenic. It's the kind of thing a pathologist would know."

"What made you take the polish off?"

"We routinely examine fingernails since they can indicate all kinds of disorders. But these were just a little different. Lots of cadavers have fingernail polish when they come to us, but it's usually not so neat as Ella's. Usually there are chips and scratches in the polish, but Ella's polish was a shellac that requires ultraviolet light to set, and there weren't any scratches, not even under the microscope. Now who does a shellac manicure on a deathly sick woman unless it's to cover something up?"

"Is arsenic what killed her?"

"Well, it contributed to her death, but it wasn't the felling blow, so to speak."

"So what's the story? How long had she been consuming arsenic?"

"Both her nails and her air showed chronic sub-acute arsenic poisoning for at least four months. It stays deposited in keratin and can be detected fairly easily. (It also stays in bone, but that's harder to test for.) The longest hairs on her head averaged four inches, and the entire lengths had demonstrable amounts of arsenic. Average hair growth is less than one inch per month, although quite a few people do grow at least an inch, so at least four months, and probably more. Hard to pinpoint without more information."

"What were her symptoms likely to have been?"

"Dizziness, really bad headaches, diarrhea, stomach pain, muscle pain and cramping, darkened skin. It ends up affecting all systems, so the symptoms are diverse, and arsenic poisoning is hard to diagnose. It can cause vitamin-A deficiency leading to heart problems, and the liver is often affected. Chronic low doses, say from natural environmental contamination, can result in cancer. I found a few small lesions on her liver and on the bottoms of her feet."

"But that didn't kill her?" Garnet wanted to know more.

"No. I'll tell you in a minute," Rachel raised one finger to indicate there was more to the story. I requested her medical records, and she was taking hydrocodone for the pain. She had arthritis too. She had been boosted up from 5.0-325 to 7.5-325 in February, something else that makes me think the poisoning was more than four months."

"So, did she overdose on hydrocodone?"

"Hydrocodone plus another very strong opiate, fentanyl."

"Fentanyl? Her doctor prescribed fentanyl on top of the hydrocodone?"

"No. I couldn't find it in her medical records, so I called her physician, Dr. Porter. He swears he never prescribed fentanyl for Ella. He has prescribed it on occasion for nursing home patients with terminal cancer, but otherwise he uses other analgesics."

"What then?" Garnet urged Rachel on.

"I almost missed it. There was a small abrasion on Ella's right thigh that looked like it might have been made from a medical patch. Older people often do not do well with patch medications because they tend to abrade the thinner skin. Garnet nodded her head in understanding. "So I cut out a small piece of the abraded skin (she showed Garnet a set of photos) and sent it over to Hattie (the lab's Director of Forensics) along with the hair and nail samples. It took her two days to run it. She had to macerate the tissue and try several solvents. That's what took so long. Sure enough, it was fentanyl, and a very high dose at that, probably 75-100 micrograms. Somebody went to a lot of trouble to set up Ella's death."

"How did Hattie determine such a high dose?"

"Because fentanyl concentrates in the skin before it crosses into the capillaries. It continues to be absorbed for as much as 24 hours. But she was dead."

"Oh, I see," Garnet had figured it out. "When her heart stopped, her circulation stopped, so there was no gradient to move the fentanyl, so it simply stayed in the skin, with limited local diffusion since it needs a patch to deliver it."

"You got it."

"So it was homicide?"

"I'm afraid so."

Garnet shook her head in disbelief. Homicide. "How? Who?" she asked Rachel.

"Well, you know that's not my job, but I'd start with the nursing staff, somebody who saw her every day."

I met Hannah Gibson, the Director of Nursing, when I went out to ask about Ella. She wasn't there when Ella died. Unless she went on vacation then snuck back in to put the patch on, then take it off as soon as Ella quit breathing, I can't see her as the killer."

"No, probably not her, but she could have done the arsenic dosing. An RN named Patricia Lewis signed the death certificate as natural causes. Whoever investigates this will want to talk to her."

"OK, I get it," Garnet was thinking out loud. "But why would you have her cremated then bury the cremains? That makes no sense to me."

"I'm not sure either. It's possible that the killer is just paranoid."

Garnet remembered the other boxes with names on them. "Do you think the other cremains in those boxes that Uncle ADD dug up would have arsenic in them?"

"I'd say that it's worth looking at. But you know I can't test them without a specific order. You'll have to take them to whoever the investigator is. He or she can make a request."

21

Garnet obsessed about the homicide finding all weekend. When Uncle ADD and Beulah came by for their usual lunch after services on Saturday, Garnet found she had trouble focusing on the conversation. Uncle ADD was describing how he had located the discarded moonstone and how he had prayed over it until he was sure The Lord Almighty didn't mind if he and Beulah gave it a try. The main problem was that they had to wait more than three weeks for a full moon.

After the two left, both Garnet and Mica graded papers and made class notes for next week's classes. It wasn't until she was getting ready for bed that Garnet remembered she had promised to go visit Maynard tomorrow. Garnet was itching to go back out to Golden Rod Acres, but she didn't have a plan for information gathering and realized she'd better stay out of Ella's death. Still, Maynard struck her as a consummate gossip, and perhaps she'd learn something after all. Besides it would be fun to see what unusual concoction Maynard had prepared for dessert.

Garnet could tell when she first arrived that something about Maynard was different. Maynard seemed nervous and kept glancing through her spying window toward the assisted care facility. Perhaps she had a rendezvous with her ex-husband later.

Garnet was taken aback when Maynard pulled the curtains closed and said in a lowered voice, "I've got somethin' to show you." When they were seated in the tiny living room, Maynard pulled out a plastic card. "Here, take a look at this," she passed the card to Garnet. It was a debit card with George Tanner's name on it.

"Does this mean you and George are seeing each other?" Garnet asked innocently.

"No, not at all!" Maynard seemed shocked at the very idea. "No. The other day, Rose Cassidy was in the Rec room with this big Fed Ex folder just stuffed with papers. She was leanin' over talkin' to Mary Swanson when a whole bunch of cards fell out. I swear, she looked like a scared rabbit, and she sure bent over to pick them up in a big hurry. I scuttled over to help her, but when I saw this one, I put my foot over it and hid it," she showed Garnet a debit card for George Tanner. "Now me and George aren't exactly seein' each other, as you put it, but we're still on friendly terms, so I thought I'd take it down to him, thinkin' it would be a nice gesture on my part."

"Well, is he going to let you run errands, or use it yourself?" Garnet was curious.

"Well, he got real huffy. And he asked me where I got that card. Then he went and got his wallet and showed me he still had his card. I was blunderbusted. But he said he figured it was just so they could pay for his medicine when they picked it up for him.

"Can you believe anybody could be that stupid? He used to be a smart man. It's for sure he isn't now. Anyway, I kept the card because I knew you'd be able to tell me what to do with it. I heard that that new black detective from the sheriff's office came out here a askin' about Ella Justice."

Garnet was seldom at a loss for words. She knew what Maynard had was important evidence in the identity theft investigation, and possibly in the homicide. Then she had a brain storm! She had come out here hoping Maynard would have some good gossip. But Maynard had gone one better. She had some important, concrete evidence that needed to go to whoever was going to investigate Ella's case. And, since she probably had any number of little tidbits tucked away, and since she could actually act as an informant without raising any suspicion, she was perfect for the unexalted position of CI!

"I tell you what," Garnet offered. "I think this is really important, and the sheriff's office is going to want to hear your story. Think of yourself as a kind of confidential informant (CI). I think somebody will want to look into this. But," she raised a finger in caution, "you need to do this on the QT.

Don't let anyone else know what you're doing, not even George," (*or you might start getting some arsenic yourself*).

"You mean especially not George," Maynard responded. "That man is dumber than a rock. He'd tell everybody. The only reason he hasn't yet is because I told him I'd take that card back to Rose Cassidy myself."

Maynard stuffed the card away in a hidden compartment in her purse and turned to Garnet as if their conversation had never occurred. "Well, did you tell your husband about the vinegar pie?" she picked up from their last visit. "I know he'll like what I made today. There'll be a little left, and you can take him some. Aren't very many people who'll turn down my molten lava cakes."

Maynard was right. The gooey chocolate was divine! Garnet thought about hiding the extra piece from Mica and having seconds all to herself.

When Garnet got home, she reluctantly handed the piece of molten lava cake over to Mica who devoured it before she had a chance to beg a bite. Then she went into the back storage area to retrieve the boxes of cremains. As soon as she found out who at the sheriff's office picked up Ella's homicide case, she'd arrange to deliver the boxes in case they were related.

Monday morning, she called the sheriff's office as soon as she got to work and asked for the detective in charge of Ella Justice's homicide. She was a little early on that. Neither the receptionist nor the young administrative assistant had a clue. Both women mentioned that Marshall Boggs was involved with Ella's identity theft case, but they had no knowledge of any homicide. Garnet promised to call back later and went to her first lecture.

22

Marshall Boggs was having a rough Monday. Sheriff Curly McCurly had given Marshall the heads up last night. The medical examiner hadn't ruled Ella's death a homicide until late Friday afternoon, so the case hadn't been assigned. All the paper work would wait until Monday. There wasn't any emergency since the victim had died over five months ago. Marshall was an excellent detective, and since he was already looking at identity theft for the victim, Curly thought combining the cases might save time. There was no guarantee that the murderer and the thief were the same, considering how many people passed through Golden Rod Acres on a regular basis. Still, since an escalation in theft occurred immediately after the death, the odds were in that direction.

As soon as Marshall walked through the door, the receptionist and the administrative assistant cornered him. He held up his hands, palms forward, as if to stand them off then invited them to join him in the conference room (where he knew coffee was located) for an update on the case. The medical examiner's findings had been transferred officially to the sheriff's office since the victim had died in Pope County, but outside city limits.

It was after 3:00 when Marshall finally caught Garnet at her desk. She explained that she had some unusual evidence she needed to show him. Hopefully it could shed some light on Ella Justice's homicide. But because the evidence was unusual, she needed to talk to him face-to-face. She got the idea that he really didn't want to talk to her today, but he sighed and promised to see her at 4:30.

When Garnet arrived promptly at 4:30, Detective Boggs was MIA. The receptionist assured her that he was finishing up some business on another case and would come out to get her in "just a few minutes". When He finally showed up half an hour later, Garnet was grinding her teeth. *The man must think he is an MD*, she snarked to herself.

The wrong foot did not become the right foot any time soon. Boggs escorted her to his postage stamp office where he began flipping through pages once he got seated. "Now, let's see," he began, not even looking at her. "You're an anatomy professor at MNSU, and you're friends with Dr. Pachebelle and Dr. West who work at the State Crime Lab. You also knew the deceased, Ella Justice, because she worked in the Anatomy Department for six years." He looked up. "Is that correct?"

"Yes," Garnet nodded her head. "And..."

He cut her off. "Tell me, Ms., uh, Daniels," he consulted his notes.

"That's Dr. Daniels," she corrected him.

"Oh, yes I am sorry," he apologized and actually looked straight at her. "Dr. Daniels, tell me again how you found out the victim was dead and why you thought identity theft had occurred, which was where I came in."

"I knew Ella was dead when her corpse showed up on a table in our Gross Anatomy course. Dr. Bradshaw and I both recognized her even though she came in under a different name. We guessed that there had been a mix-up at the funeral home, especially considering that the Johnny twins were involved."

"Yes," he commented dryly, "I've met the Johnny twins. Sorry about that."

"Ms. Justice, or the deceased, as you say, had run our donated body program when she was with us and had signed the paperwork to donate her body. However, we cannot use a body unless we have a death certificate. We had the other woman's death certificate. So, I went to Bach Brothers in Dover to get a copy of the death certificate since that was where the body had been. When I got out there, Mr. Bach showed me Ella's file pointing out that she had been assigned to cremation."

Boggs jumped in again, "but that didn't make sense, did it?"

"No, and especially when you see the evidence I brought. To continue, I went out to Golden Rod Acres to sleuth a little, if you will." He lifted one eyebrow but signaled for her to continue. "They told me she had deteriorated very quickly and had died before they could transfer her to a nursing home. The Director of Nursing told me she had been on vacation when Ella died, but her nonverbal indicated some conflict. The official story was that Ella had no known relatives, so she was cremated, and her ashes were scattered in the memory garden."

"Did she have any relatives?"

"Only one that I knew of, her niece, Dr. Scarlett Mars, who signed the identity theft complaint."

"And, what made her think that her aunt's identity had been stolen?"

Garnet knew he already had that information, but she continued anyway, "when she went to the lockbox that her aunt had left for her, it had been cleaned out. She had a copy of the will, so she was able to find the lawyer and executor of the estate, Tom Wiseman." Boggs nodded to indicate he knew Wiseman. "Tom had Ella's accounts frozen immediately. When the account printouts finally came, it was clear someone had been drawing on the account. Tom sent Scarlett over here to file an identity theft complaint."

Marshall Boggs looked at Garnet and broke into a Cheshire Cat smile. "Wow, you make a better case than I do. You sat here and in 10 minutes and told me what it had taken me hours to piece together by myself. I need you working for me! Were you also on the trail that led to the discovery of homicide?"

"Yes and no. I really didn't expect homicide, but I just couldn't accept 'natural causes'. I had Scarlett request an autopsy. I knew that since identity theft had been pretty well established, Dr. Pachebelle would do the autopsy. And there is nobody so thorough as she is."

"I'm beginning to learn that. I was really impressed with her arsenic findings. And diluting fentanyl from the skin where a patch had been was a stroke of genius. But you said you had additional evidence?"

"Are you sure you have time for this?" Garnet noticed it was already 5:30. He nodded, and she started in again by opening up the black bag and placing the six boxes in a row on his desk with the names facing him.

"These are what you call cremains?" he asked hoping he had the correct term.

"Yes they are. And look at the names."

He noticed Ella Justice's name straight off and pulled her box toward him for closer examination. "This is the same Ella Justice whose ashes have been spread in the memorial gardens at Golden Rod Acres and the same Ella Justice whose body is now at the State Crime Lab?"

Garnet nodded. "That's what got me started in the first place. When I found out Ella had been poisoned and that the whole cremation thing was way off, I started wondering if there were any others. Since arsenic binds to bones, even after cremation, it should still be detectible. So I thought we ought to get these cremains tested. Then Rachel, Dr. Pachobelle, told me she couldn't test them on my say. She needed an official chain of evidence."

Marshall took a deep breath. "Yes I can see that, but speaking of chain of evidence, where did you get these?"

"I knew you were going to ask me that. You haven't been here very long, have you?"

"About nine months."

"Well," she took a deep breath, "have you heard about my uncle, ADD?"

23

Marshall went in to work early Tuesday. His head was full of bits of information and lots of questions that needed to be organized before this dual investigation got away from him. He started making a list. He needed to talk to Tom Wiseman, who was executor of Ms. Justice's will; and he needed to talk to Dr. Scarlett Mars who was the beneficiary of the will and who kept a key to the empty lockbox. He needed to call Dr. Daniels to get Dr. Mars' number. It was a big intertwined pattern that connected all these people. Dr. Daniels knew Dr. West and Dr. Pachebelle at the State Crime Lab, and all three women had known the deceased as had the lawyer and the niece. Then there was this crazy Uncle ADD person who was running around at the full moon digging up buried treasure he found with a moonstone. And the cemetery site, who had buried those boxes of cremains in the first place?

He was finishing up the paper work to send the cremains to the State Crime Lab for arsenic poisoning when the receptionist buzzed him. "You have a visitor out here who wants to talk to you alone. She won't tell me what it's about, but she said a Dr. Garnet Daniels sent her."

Marshall took more than one deep breath before telling the receptionist to send the woman back. There was a little red flag waving in his brain. What in the world were these women up to?

Maynard glanced from side to side as she walked down the short hall to Marshall's office and nervously took a seat that was a little behind the door as if she were hiding form someone. She leaned forward just slightly and blurted out, "I'm Maynard Tanner, and I'm your confidential informant!"

Marshall's eyes widened and he scrutinized her carefully, "you're my what?"

"Your confidential informant," she replied sincerely. "That's what Miss Garnet told me I could be. She said you'd need a confidential informant out at Golden Rod Acres."

He contemplated throwing the woman out then calling **Dr.** Daniels to give her a piece of his mind. Then he remembered the pattern of interconnection between these women and their relatives and friends. He decided to go for it, "and just what did you want to inform me about today?" Good Lord, he hadn't even made it back to Golden Rod Acres, and here was someone trying to give him information!

Marshall stood up and closed the door, watching Maynard visibly relax. He motioned her to the chair beside his cluttered desk and gave her a questioning look. As she moved to the nearby chair, she rummaged in her giant purse and pulled a zipper bag holding a green and black bank card.

"I brought you this," she handed him the card.

"He circled his hand to indicate that she should continue. "Tell me why I need this card."

"Because it's a fake."

He examined it carefully. It was an ATM/debit card from a local bank with the name George Tanner on it. It looked perfectly fine.

"And how do you know it's a fake?"

"Because he still has the real one."

"OK," he was going to have to ask more specific questions. "You'd better tell me straight out why this card is a fake and how you came by it."

Maynard was happy to oblige. She told him the same story she told Garnet about putting her foot over it when it was dropped and taking it back to George himself. "Me and him, I'm sorry, he and I used to be married a long time ago, but we still get along all right. Now that he's in assisted care, I kind of watch out for him. You know how it is."

No, he didn't know, but he wasn't about to let that stop him. All kinds of bells were going off in his logic system. "So somebody had this card made without his knowledge?"

When she nodded twice, he continued. "When would he have given his original card to someone?"

"Oh, that's easy. Lots of folks in assisted livin' get medicine or ask for little things when the courtesy van makes a trip. They give the driver their cards to pay for things, and they always get them back. Or," she continued, "people are all the time losin' their cards or leavin' them at the snack bar. Or," there was more, "not hardly anyone locks a door out there. I could steal a few things myself if I'd a mind to."

Marshall devised a plan, which he thought was very clever, for his "confidential informant" to contact him through Garnet. And if he needed to ask her something or warn her, he would communicate through Garnet too. There was no way this little surprise would go unacknowledged.

After Maynard left, looking carefully from side to side, Marshall filled out the paper work for the duplicated card to go the Arkansas Crime lab along with the bones. Could there be more victims? He thought about the cards he had been given by Rose Cassidy last week. Could they all be counterfeit? He filled out more paperwork for those cards to be examined as well. It wasn't much evidence, but they had to start somewhere.

Late in the afternoon, Garnet got a call from Marshall Boggs requesting Scarlett's phone number. "Anything else?" she asked politely.

"I was going to ask you the same thing," he was a little gruffer than he had intended. "I met my confidential informant this morning, and I was wondering if you had any more surprises for me."

Garnet quickly figured out that Maynard had taken the bull by the horns. "Oh, I am so sorry," she apologized, knowing there was really no excuse for not giving him a heads up. She had simply forgotten. "I guess you're really pissed at me. My bad. I should have warned you. But no, I don't have anything else just now. Mica, my husband is helping Tom Wiseman look at Ella's financials. I'll let you know if they find anything."

Mica? Her Husband? When was this going to stop? Before long her pets would be in it too!

24

Wednesday morning, Marshall called ahead then headed back out to Golden Rod Acres to try to tie up some loose ends. Rose Cassidy had given him all those cards, but there should be more. Where was Ella's birth certificate? Where were her receipts for her assisted living care and the EOB's from Medicare and her supplement? And where were her checks and record books?

When Marshall entered the assisted care facility, the first thing that he noticed was Maynard who was playing the piano for a sing along. She looked straight at him as if she had never seen him, then winked. She was playing her part as a CI to perfection.

As she continued to play, he approached the reception desk. "Oh, hello, Marshal," the receptionist smiled brightly, not realizing that Marshall was his name, not his rank. "Miss Rose is in her office. She said to send you on back."

Marshall walked down the hall and knocked at the door. Rose looked up from her desk, clearly very busy. She signaled for him to come in and pointed to the one empty chair. She had piles of papers and folders stacked on all the others. She ignored him and finished whatever was on her desk before looking up and speaking, "ah yes, Marshall Boggs, what brings you back out here?"

He gathered from her demeanor that she really didn't want to talk to him, but that was her problem, not his. "We are still missing several of Ella Justice's effects. And I was hoping you could help us. What happens to a person's belongings when the room is cleaned out?"

"Well, we box them up and send them along to wherever they are going.

Most go to a nursing home, but some move in with relatives. Some even go to homes out of state." She wasn't making this easy.

"Well, what about the effects of people who die here?"

"Well, we have so few, only a couple a year, you know, a heart attack or stroke, or whatever. Or sometimes you go into their rooms in the morning, and they're dead. We had fully intended to get Ella moved to nursing before she died. I hope her family isn't planning to sue us!" She was hoping to learn more about the one or more relatives who were involved.

"No, Ma'am," he answered politely. "But we would like to know where her belongings got off to since there wasn't anyone here to claim them."

"Oh, oh," she looked at him with consternation, "I just remembered! Oh, I am so sorry. We put the rest of her things into boxes and put them into storage. We have so few deaths, and I never saw the boxes personally, that I actually forgot about them. You know, out of sight, out of mind. I am so sorry. I'll call Leon. He's our plant manager, and he can bring the boxes down for you. Of course you and I will have to go through them together to list all the contents. Or I guess you could sign for them 'as is'," she lifted her eyebrow in a question.

"Yes, I think that makes sense under the circumstances," he agreed.

She called Leon Durango to ask him how many boxes there were and whether he could bring them down or have Marshall come up to get them. "Leon says there are four or five boxes, he can't remember. They are in the locked storage area at the shop, so it would be better if you just drove up there."

"What about your receipt?"

"Oh," she seemed flustered, "I already forgot. Where is my mind? I am so busy today," she pointed to the piles of paper. She made out a receipt with the number of boxes left blank for him to fill in. Then she gave him directions to the shop where Leon was waiting.

Leon had five boxes sitting on his desk when Marshall pulled up in the SUV. They were numbered one of five, two of five, etc, so there was no reason to look for more. Marshall filled in the receipt, signed it, then had Leon sign it. Now all he had to do was go back to the office and inventory the contents.

Marshall checked his messages, took an early lunch, then started in on the boxes. Box one, the largest one, was women's clothing. Nothing there to help the cause. Box two was medical supplies: a home blood pressure kit, pulse-ox meter, Band-Aids, mouth wash, etc., all stored in candy boxes. There were also several partial vials of medications. Marshall pulled these out for further processing. He planned to take them to Dr. Pachebelle for official evaluation.

The third box was full of miscellaneous papers, pens, calendars, tape, etc. She must have had 30 ballpoints and at least 200 paperclips. There was an address book which he pulled out to go through later.

Box number four had most of what he was looking for. Her checks and check registers were in with EOBs, doctors reminders, and insurance statements, all tucked into five Whitman's Sampler boxes. Box five had some personal letters (worth looking at) and knick-knacks. She had obviously been a cat lady and there were little cat figurines, a cat covered insulated drinking cup, cat designer sheets, and any number of cat novelties. Marshal pulled the personal letters out for further perusal. They might be recent enough to give him some clue as to her state of mind.

Marshall started organizing the contents of box four, taking items out of the chocolate boxes and putting like things in piles. He put the old check registers and bank statements into one pile along with her unused checks. Since Tom Wiseman and Mica Manfreid had the chore of unraveling Ella's financial records, he called Tom and offered to drop them off later in the afternoon. Then he called the State Crime Lab and arranged to drop off the medications for Dr. Pachebelle. The assistant who took his call requested that he also bring all Ella's vitamins and supplements so a search for counter-indicated combinations could be made. Someone would be at the lab late, and he could combine his two trips.

Meanwhile, Marshall perused the stack of personal correspondence, sorting back to the first of the year. There was a late Christmas greeting and short letter from Scarlett, telling her aunt she was on her way to Davis, but would return to Fayetteville in late summer and would see her then. Most of the letters were just chit chat between friends. But there was an unfinished letter that Ella had started in February:

Dear Eileen,

I've been meaning to write to you, but have been sick for a while. I never even got my Christmas Cards out this year. I just feel so dizzy, and my stomach hurts all the time. The doctor assures me that it isn't an ulcer, but I've been drinking butter milk anyway. He also upped my hydrocodone medicine because I've been really achy and sore all over.

So, she had been sick since before Christmas. He'd mention that when he dropped the medications off.

When Marshall made his second stop to drop off the financial records, Tom and Mica were waiting for him, eager to see what useful pieces of information they could glean from the new papers. Marshall told them he still had some loose ends to run down on his side of the investigation Thursday, and they agreed to meet Friday evening at Tom's for pizza and to review loose ends with the goal of untangling the financial picture of Ella's last months.

25

Marshall finished up his paper work Thursday morning then spent some time on the internet trying to find out as much as he could about the Galley Creek Cemetery before he drove out there that afternoon. It wasn't that he didn't believe Garnet. It was that he couldn't believe her. He could just hear the guffaws when he tried to explain to a judge that the bones in question had been dug up and removed from Galley Creek Cemetery because an elderly man and his girlfriend and a friend with a moonstone had driven there because Jesse James had appeared to the woman to tell her to go there because something important was buried near one of the graves.

Marshall took HWY-105 south at Atkins and jogged at the old depot to continue south. He knew he had not seen anything that looked like a cemetery before he reached the Sweeden Island Park. Luckily he had the number of a local resident who had organized Galley Rock History Day back about 10 years ago. The directions were pretty much as the crow flies. He was to go past a field of round hay bales on the right where the trees were cut out into a vee. Then he needed to go to the next field of hay bales, about a mile, and there it was on the right.

Marshall almost missed it again, but he pulled in beside an historical Galley Rock marker on the highway, and there to his right was the cemetery! It was on a big hill with a low chain link fence surrounding it. The double gates appeared to be chained and padlocked, but a single gate on the left was standing open.

He fished out his camera and began to climb the steep hill. Higher up on the hill on the north end, two tombstones with spires, one about twice the size of the other, stood beneath a giant oak tree. As he walked along the ridge of the hill moving slowly south, he saw various old tombstones scattered here and there. He was surprised because he had expected neat rows and well marked family plots. He came upon a plot with several tomb stones surrounded by a metal fence. This couldn't be what he was looking for because there were no top spikes in the fence. Instead the metal had been formed into small, fingerlike columns with filigrees of wire connecting them. It reminded him of the hairpin lace his mother used to crochet. Over on another rise of the hill, he found what he was looking for. There was a plot with several large and two or three small, maybe 10" x 12" tombstones enclosed in a tall metal fence with pointed posts. This had to be the one Garnet had described based on what the girlfriend had told her.

It was easy to enter the plot. Someone had left the gate wide open. Marshall entered and carefully surveyed the ground. Quite a few oak leaves had blown into the square, and he didn't see any disturbance in the dirt until he brushed some of the leaves into a pile. There it was right in the center of the plot as advertised, a shallow hole about 30" square. Something had been taken out of the plot not so very long ago.

Marshall continued his tour of the rocky hill up above the Arkansas River looking for other signs that the dirt had been disturbed. He found none. The cemetery had an abandoned, yet peaceful, feel to it as if the deceased had moved away long ago. The last recorded burial had been in 1900, over 100 years ago. Since then, the people and their personas had vanished into history.

The large, rocky burial site evoked images of Sinclair Lewis' *Our Town*, with people from the valley carrying their dead up to a safe place on the steep hill. Galley (Galla) Rock had once been a river port and trading village, first established by the Cherokee in Arkansas Territory in the early 1800s. Galley Rock did not become a town until 1835 after the Cherokee had moved farther west into Oklahoma. In 1840 as many as 217 people, according to the census, lived there at the bottom of the hill, closer to the river where they made their living mostly by farming the rich river bottoms.

When the railroad passed north of the little town in the 1870s, it began to dwindle and was gone by 1900, leaving only the Galley Rock Cemetery as a witness to its existence.

Marshall was stymied. Someone knew about this lonely cemetery and had come here to bury those boxes of bones. There was no real reason to suspect that the person(s) in question were descendants of the folks at Galley Rock. And there was still no explanation as to why the bones had been buried in the first place. Why not just sprinkle them in the river? Perhaps they were trophies of some kind.

26

Thursday was a really bad day for Nurse Hannah. She was listening to, more than watching, the morning news when she heard something that riveted her to the screen. Dimitri Popolov, a sophisticated cybercriminal had been arrested in Miami, Florida. There on the TV was a video of Dimitri in cuffs being escorted by two men in suits into the court building in Las Vegas.

The cable station put a still picture of Dimitri on the screen then continued the story. Dimitri Popolov was the head of a $60 million theft ring. His organized group had stolen and duplicated credit cards and debit cards to quickly wipe out bank accounts. His professional hackers had breached at least two credit/debit processing companies to steal card numbers. Those cards had been used in every state in the union to steal over $10 million, mostly from ATMs. He had been laundering money through a group of small businesses in Miami.

The current investigation was being handled by federal prosecutors who were rounding up Popolov's known associates. A high ranking associate, Laurenz Esteban, had been arrested in Richmond, Virginia. Esteban was responsible for producing millions of dollars in fake documents for illegal immigrants. Popolov was facing up to 60 years in prison, and Esteban, 20 years.

Hannah was so shocked that she crumbled onto the couch with her mouth open. How could this be? She knew Dimitri had been laundering money, but $60 million? She had no idea what the scope of his business was. Thankfully, even knowing that her own little shop was clean, she had pulled away eight years ago getting herself and Randi away from something that had begun to smell rotten.

But was she safe? The feds would have Dimitri's records as far back they could go. Tax records would show Dimitri as the owner of her shop. Her own tax returns showed her as the shop manager. Then there was the generous trust fund he had set up for Randi when she graduated or turned 25. And, he had paid the balance of her tuition and fees at Talequa. She had a nice scholarship, but not a full ride. Cross country runners weren't high enough up on the pecking order to get a full ride, even if they were stronger students than many of the football jocks.

Hannah used one of her burner phones to call Randi. Was her land line tapped? Did they think she might lead them to someone else? That sheriff's deputy had been out here twice now. What was he after? She got voice mail and left a short cryptic message. "Randi, Pop-Pop is very ill. Take care of yourself so you don't catch it too."

Hannah went to her office looking back over her shoulder, fully expecting FBI agents to pop out of the woodwork. She was already paranoid enough to put a flat toothpick between the outer door and sill. As soon as she sat down, she went through her mind identifying the people who had a key that would access her house. Several people had keys to this building, but only Rose Cassidy and Leon Durango, the plant supervisor had a key to every building.

Leon! Oh dear. Leon was not a security nut. He often handed his whole key ring to someone who needed to change a filter in one of the houses. He usually drove the van to transport occupants and run errands. Hannah knew for a fact that he often left his ring on his desk while he went to town. She herself had plowed through that ring one day to unlock the pump house for a repair man. Any number of people might have a master key now. She fervently hoped none of them wanted into her house.

Hannah went past the snack bar to pick up a bottle of water before making her rounds with the residents. As she put her food card into the reader, she noticed another card lying there. "Do you know who left this?" she asked Darlene who was on duty today.

Darlene gave the card a good look then commented, "oh. yeah, that's George's. He's always leavin' his things layin' around. Would you mind takin' it back to him? I'll be gettin' busy here in a minute."

Hannah nodded and picked up the card. She started down the glassed-in hall, talking to residents along the way. When she reached George's apartment, the door was closed, so she knocked politely, then once again. There was no response, so she assumed he was out. She used the key to open the door so she could leave his card. To her surprise, there was Maynard in her underwear sitting across George's lap in his big lift chair. For his part, George was fully clothed except that his shirt was wide open and his pants were unzipped.

"Oh, excuse me! I am so sorry! I just wanted to bring George's card back to him. I knocked twice."

"Now don't go a worryin'," Maynard was completely unruffled. "Me and George is just cuddlin'. There's not a thing here that you haven't seen before."

Hannah nodded and backed out of the room, leaving the card beside the box of Russell Stover chocolates on the lamp table near the door. She didn't know whether to laugh or cry. The image of the two of them that kept coming to her mind was actually quite funny. She figured if he got tired of Maynard he could use his lift chair to dump her onto the floor. She had tried to be discreet and not stare at them, but she couldn't help noticing that George's chest was getting darker. Evidently Maynard had coaxed him out into the sun.

Later that afternoon Hannah ran into Rose Cassidy and asked her about the man from the sheriff's office. "Oh, him," Rose was nonchalant. "Would you believe it? Ella Justice had a relative after all. He was out here trying to find all of her effects. I gave him her cards out of the vault last week, but I forgot all about her stuff in storage until he came back asking this week. I would have given Ella's things to her family," she said petulantly. "I don't know why they had to send the law out here." She was quite huffy.

When Hannah went home that evening, the toothpick was still in the door. What a relief!

She sat down for a while to gather herself then started fixing a snack. She wasn't hungry enough to fix a regular meal. She was just about to bite into her turkey sandwich when the call from Randi came in on the burner phone.

"Hi, Mom, what's up with Pop-pop? I got the idea he might be a little more than sick."

"He was on the news this morning being arrested. They finally caught the old fox."

"Oh, man, I hate that. Is that going to be a problem for us?"

"I don't think so, but I'm being cautious. They're trying to round up his associates, and they might come here. As far as I know we're clean. You know we left there eight years ago to get you, and me too, away from that mess. But he has paid your college expenses so you can run cross-country and not have to work.

"Yeah, I hadn't thought about that," Randi was sympathetic.

"And," Hannah continued, "he did set up your trust fund. In the worst case scenario, we may have to forfeit that. Let's wait and see. Just don't make any unusual or large purchases for awhile. Understand?"

Later, when she turned on the late night news out of Little Rock, Dimitri's arrest was mentioned again since he had criminal ties to many other states, including Arkansas.

27

Mica was busy sorting spreadsheets into piles on the big table when Garnet came into the kitchen Friday morning. "Got a project report today?" she inquired.

"Yes. I guess you could say that. Marshall dropped off some more of Ella's bank records yesterday, and I've been trying to incorporate them into what we already had."

"And?"

"Some things are clearer. Some are not. We're meeting today at 4:00 at Tom's. Want to join us?"

"I may be able to drop in after 5:00. If I can, I'll call to take dinner orders." She filled her cup with coffee and creamer while he loaded his briefcase and headed out the door.

"Is Scarlett coming tonight?" he paused at the door.

"No, not until we have a better picture or need information only she might have."

On her way to work, Garnet kept thinking about the boxes of cremains, hoping Rachel would be getting a report on their arsenic content today. The Arkansas Crime Lab didn't have the equipment to do the assay in bone, so the samples had to be sent out via overnight express. If the data didn't come in today, it would be next week sometime before the report arrived.

The cremains presented a bit of a slippery slope. Garnet fully expected arsenic to be discovered in some of the samples, but not necessarily all. She reasoned that the bones in the box labeled "Ella Justice" were actually those of Ms. Summermann, who, coming from a different facility, logically would not have been poisoned with arsenic. Unfortunately, if arsenic were found in any of the other samples, that would not be reliable evidence of cause of death. After all, Ella's cause of death was from an overdose of fentanyl with arsenic poisoning and heavy doses of hydrocodone as contributing factors. Still, Garnet was excited about the possible results.

Nurse Hannah took a break from work and walked up the dusty hill to the maintenance building where Leon was also taking a break (if he ever actually had done any work). He motioned her in out of the heat and offered her some cold bottled water as he continued to sip on his own drink. They chit chatted a bit (one of the local areas rituals) then she became more direct. "Leon, You've just got to tell me what that sheriff's deputy was doing out here this week. He was here last week too. What's the local gossip?"

Leon took a big swig of his orange colored drink then wiped his mouth with the back of his hand. He looked furtively around the room as if hidden spies were likely to be there behind the shelves of tools. "You mean Wednesday when he was out here?" he clarified. "He come up here to get the last of Miss Ella's things. There's somethin' about somebody showing up as a long lost relative and askin' all kinds of questions about how she died."

"Well, I saw him last week, and he was talking to Rose Cassidy," she was fishing. Rose talked to Leon more than she did to anybody else.

"Now I asked her about that, and she said he had come for Ella's credit card and bank card and had not breathed a word about wantin' anything else. She was pretty miffed at him because he left the impression that she had been holdin' out on him about this other stuff. But that most certainly was not the case," he was quick to defend her. "Miss Rose said she simply forgot, what with him showin' up like that out of the blue without any warning or nothin'."

"Did he say what he was looking for?"

"Not as far as Miss Rose and I could tell. He seemed to be interested purely in Ella's financials. Now if it was me, I'd a wanted to know about her health. How come that no good family of hers let her lay out here by herself 'til she died?"

Exactly, thought Hannah to herself. *Her financials and her health. What did I miss? What really happened here?*

Marshall Boggs was looking forward to this afternoon's meeting with Tom and Mica. What information he had gathered this week led him toward thinking the homicide and the identity theft were the same case. Nevertheless until he had a definite link, he would treat this as two cases. He pulled out a pad and began jotting down knowns, unknowns, and find-outs.

The homicide part produced a short list. Ella died on March 26 of an overdose of fentanyl augmented with hydrocodone and arsenic; fentanyl and arsenic administered by person, or persons, unknown. Evidence suggested that Ella first became ill around Christmas time. Continuation and worsening of her symptoms led to increased strength of hydrocodone doses. Then she had been administered a lethal dose, or a dose that proved to be lethal, of fentanyl.

He hadn't looked closely at the bank records he had retrieved Wednesday. He was hoping Tom and Mica had a handle on that so they could all agree on the next steps to take. He was almost ready to leave when Rachel Pachebelle called. The results from the bone samples had just been faxed to her. Five of the six samples tested positive for quantities of arsenic consistent with poisoning. The negative sample, as expected, was from the subject believed to be Ms. Summermann.

The phone was ringing as he gathered his papers to leave. *Just head out the door, and the phone will ring*, he thought to himself. To his surprise it was Gracie. "Hey there," she started out familiarly, "Guess who just got out of her church decorating job. I know you probably already have other plans, but I thought I'd give it a try."

"No, no," he stuttered, "I hadn't made other plans, but I do have an important meeting that might run as late as seven. Will you still be hungry by then?" Damn! He had forgotten about asking her out Wednesday when he was at Golden Rod Acres.

"Will I be hungry? I'll be famished. You might have to scrape me off the floor."

"I might be able to do that," he laughed. "How about I pick you up, say, about 7:30, in case the meeting runs long. You go ahead and get yourself a little snack before then. OK? He wrote down her address and took her phone number off CID then headed out the door again.

28

Tom Wiseman was just locking up his cabinets when Marshall arrived, and Mica came through the door a few minutes later. Tom allowed each man to pick a drink from his little cooler then led them back to the conference room. Mica relayed Garnet's offer to pick up some dinner later.

"I'll have to pass on that. I have a daa..., um, meeting later this evening, so I'll have to leave here by 6:30," Marshall explained. I think I have the homicide fairly well outlined if you want me to start there. Right now the data set is considerably shorter than the one for the identity theft." He handed a copy of his summary and questions to each man.

> "Victim: Ella Gene Justice
>   Assisted Living Resident at Golden Rod Acres (GRA)
>
> Date of death: May 26, 2018 at about 2:30 am
> COD: Fentanyl overdose via patch; arsenic poisoning and hydrocodone as contributing factors
>
> First tier questions:
>   – who inside and/or outside has regular contact with residents
>   – who inside/outside has regular medical contact with residents
>   – who was at GRA that day and night
>   – how was the arsenic given

- what about other residents as suspects
- who has keyed access to front and back doors of suites

Related questions:
- who has master keys
- who was in the building that day and night
- who is Patricia Lewis, the RN on duty that night
- did Rose Cassidy have a nursing home bed lined up for the victim

On the bottom of the page he had written the newest information, *Rachel Pachebelle: 5 of 6 bone samples positive for arsenic. Must pull as much info as poss about each subject, including death certificates and financials*

Since the victimology was well established, the men moved on to the first tier questions. Marshall took the lead. "We know that the people who run the place had regular contact. That would be the director, Rose Cassidy; the social worker, Gracie Preston; the Director of Nursin', Hannah Farris; maybe Leon Durango; maybe kitchen and cleaning staff; and, of course, from time to time, Nurse Patricia Lewis. There have to be family and church members who visit regularly, but I'm goin' to leave them until we've figured out these others. We also know that various medical doctors came by on some kind of regular basis. Residents relied mostly on the APN, Hannah, but nurses in Arkansas can't prescribe opioids."

He stopped and took a long drag on his Mt Dew, then continued. "I don't think we can nail down who was at GRA that day and night except for the major players. We know Nurse Patricia Lewis was there. She signed the death certificate. We'll have to find her and interview her. We think we know that Nurse Hannah Gibson was not there that night. She had been on vacation for three days with Lewis fillin' in. I'll have to go back out there to find out about keys. All those suites have a little patio thing out the back. The front along the glassed in hall is likely to be well lit at night. I'll have to find out more about the keys and the night lights. I also need to find out how many master keys are out there floatin' around. Man, this place is security hell.

"As to how the arsenic was administered, I have no real idea. It must have gone in by mouth, but what was it in and how was it disguised? Your guess is as good as mine. I think we covered most of these related questions on the way through. But, call me a cynic, I have to ask if there ever was an arrangement for the victim to be transferred to a nursing home. That could be a pivotal question. And, where are the donated body forms? She had them at one time or she wouldn't be registered at MNSU. Did anyone out there know she had donated her body? I'll look through all her papers again and ask my CI."

"CI?" Tom asked. "How did you get a CI out there?"

"Don't ask. Mica, it was your wife that sent her to me."

"Garnet? How'd she do that?"

"Well, it seems Garnet has been visitin' a lady out there who has big eyes and ears. Garnet told her she could be my CI, and damned if she didn't show up at my office!"

"Is she any good?" Tom wondered.

"Yes she is." Marshall pulled George's debit card out of his file and explained that it had been duplicated. "I was going to give this to you guys because it's related to the identity theft situation."

29

"OK, I guess I'm next," Tom volunteered. "Unfortunately I still have more questions than answers. What we do know is that someone had a key to the lockbox and stole Ella's passport and an elk's tooth and whatever else was there, maybe even the donated body forms. We know that someone, possibly Ella, began regular weekly withdrawals of $300 in January and that there was a jump to a weekly $600 beginning in April, after her death. We had assumed that her own card were being used. But now that we know George's card had been duplicated, who's to say? Marshall, those cards of Ella's that you brought us may all be duplicates!"

"We've been looking at her monthly income and expenses before and after her death." Mica picked up the story. She had $3,000 from her trust fund, $1,333 from Social Security, and $1,625 from Arkansas State Retirement, all by direct deposit, for a total of $5,958. Her Golden Rod package, including just about all her expenses was $4,084, paid by direct deposit. That left her $874 monthly for herself, or a little over $200 a week.

"She wrote a monthly check for $150 to her church and another for $75 to Food 4 Kids. Then she'd write checks for $25 to one or more charities each month. She took out about $300 cash each month and kept a balance of about $300 from month to month.

"Then, when she died, and the deposit to GRA was stopped, she had the entire $5,958 every month. Starting in April, someone began drawing $600 weekly with her debit card and making monthly minimum payments to her credit card accounts, total about $75. The kicker is a monthly check for $3,300 to *Golden Card Company*. The result is that somebody was bleeding Ella's account for almost $6,000 a month!

"OK," he continued, "We know that our ID-thief was a good forger and a good impersonator. The lockbox was emptied before Ella died. We don't know if her checks were all forged, or if she did what many old folks do--sign a bunch of blank checks for somebody else to fill out. I'm guessing forgery because the numbers jumped after March, and there are some checks missing from those you brought us. There are no checks written after the day Tom had the account frozen, and we know someone tried to use Ella's debit card that night. Whoever it was knew the game was up at that point."

At this point, Marshall checked his watch, "Uh, sorry guys, but I'm goin' to have to leave pretty soon. Looks like we have a jillion data requests. And it looks like I'll have to make them. OK, I'll get background checks right away for the main players, and let's add the social worker, Gracie Preston. She's been under our radar, and that might be important. (*That'll cover my ass about dating her.*) Then I'll request employment records from GRA Corporate. We need these for both cases. There may be some clues in our players pasts. And, of course, I'll see what I can learn about our arsenic contaminated cremains friends."

Marshall was heading out the door when Garnet called to take dinner orders. When she arrived with tuna subs, apples and Cheetos, they ate and crunched, then started again, kicking ideas around. "The more I think about it," Mica started, "the more sure I am that the *Golden Card Company* isn't a company at all. I think somebody is building a big nest egg. Although that number 6980 on the note line does suggest another card. Whoever is running this scam is looking more and more professional."

"I was beginning to suspect that too," Tom agreed. "Oh well, back to the bank on Monday. They should have records of where the payout was sent."

30

Marshall checked his watch when he started his SUV. He had to drive from Glenwood Avenue, east to Spring Lake Apartments, get cleaned up, then drive back across town to Oak Lane apartments near Legacy Lodge. He was running just a little early, so he called Gracie to give her a heads up before he left his parking lot. "Are you still ravenous?" he asked when she answered her phone.

"You bet I am!" she laughed. "If you were going to be late, I was going to be dead!"

"I should be there in about fifteen. Turn your porch light on so I can find you easier. It's the third apartment, right? And, decide where you'd like to go. My mind is too full of police work right now to make a good decision."

They ended up going to Brown's Catfish, the only seafood buffet in Russellville. They could go to a place with a bar later. Or not. They made a handsome couple and heads turned as they moved down the food bar.

She loaded her plate with you-peel-'em shrimp, and he took mostly salads, then added a huge pile of catfish fillets. "So I guess this means you're not a 'black vegetarian'," she smiled, looking at his plate.

"Oh, no, don't even go there." he shook his head sadly, unfolding his napkin. "My little sister, Taneeka, is into all that now. Sometimes I think my folks are wastin' their money sending her to LSU."

"That's a good school," she offered. "I got my social science degree from MNSU and my geriatric certification on-line from Mississippi State. I was really pleased to get my job at Golden Rod Acres. I'd been working at nursing homes. I know I was helping, but it was kind of depressing. Did you know that 80% of folks in nursing homes in Arkansas are on Medicaid?"

"I heard that most people die within six months after enterin' a nursing home. Is that true?"

"No, not really, some of them die after a month," she baited him.

He was shocked at her bad taste. But he saw the little pull on one corner of her mouth and the shining brown eyes, and realized she was teasing. "You're right," he redirected, "that's a horrible topic for a first date. We could be talkin' about Donald Trump instead."

She laughed out loud at that, and they ate in silence for a few minutes. "Do you like your work?" he asked sincerely? "You seem to get along really well with the residents. And I guess you don't see much death at Golden Rod Acres."

"I heard you were asking about Ella Justice," she caught on really quickly. "I've just been there a year, but I understand that two people died there last year, kinda like Ella. They started getting sick and died before they could be transferred to a nursing home. Now that's just our assisted care." She saw him frown. "Nobody from the rest of the retirement village. And you know some of our people," he liked that she took ownership, "have heart conditions, or have already had strokes, or whatever. They're not the healthiest population of retirees you'll find."

"Yeah," he said, "I can see that. Did you know Ella before she got sick?"

Gracie smiled, and a nostalgic look crossed her face. "Yeah, she was a classy lady. She always had her hair done, and I never saw her without fingernail polish. It wasn't like she was extravagant, or anything. She was just as nice as she could be. She was always in the Rec room visiting with the other residents and singing when Maynard played. She loved to sing. The other thing she liked was chocolate. I never saw her room without a box of chocolates, Whitman's Samplers especially. She used the boxes to store things in. She had her makeup in one on her dresser, and another with her jewelry, and one with her check book. I think she could have stored her life in Whitman's Sampler boxes!"

Time to shift the conversation before she caught on to his prying, "speaking of chocolate, they have chocolates on the ice cream bar. But the best thing in town is one of their big soft cinnamon rolls. I could eat a dozen of those."

"Oh, I know," she agreed. "That's one of the reasons I like to come here. I simply cannot leave without a cinnamon roll."

They each had one cinnamon roll then decided to be good and quit, especially since it was close to closing time already. They talked it over and decided to go down to the Front Street Grill in Dardanelle for a drink and some live music. She ordered Long Island Iced Tea, and he ordered a Margarita. The music was loud, but they pulled their chairs close together and managed to talk and flirt anyway. It was after midnight when he drove her home.

"I really had a good time tonight," he told her at the door, as he put his forehead against hers. "Could we do this again maybe?"

"Yes, I'd like that." She smiled before he kissed her gently then left, not hinting at sex or anything else. *Wow,* she thought to herself, *this could get to be pretty good!.*

31

It was a hot weekend, and many of the Golden Rod Acres residents stayed inside until late in the evening when the Rec room livened up. The heat didn't seem to hurt the attendance at the weekly Sunday brunch. Anyone in the whole complex could attend. The assisted living folks were automatically included, and the others had until Saturday afternoon to make reservations.

Hannah sat down next to Maynard who was enjoying her hash brown casserole. Suddenly Maynard blanched and started taking deep breaths. "Are you all right?" Hannah asked sympathetically.

"It's just my stomach," Maynard was patting her abdomen. "I didn't know it was going to hurt so much to get back with George. I think it's all that chocolate. He has it all over the place, and I can not stay out of it. I'm the worst kind of chocoholic. And, last Sunday I made molten lava cake. You should try it the next time I make it. I gave Miss Garnet a piece last week. She sure liked it."

"Miss Garnet? Isn't that the lady from MNSU who was out here asking about Ella?"

"Yeah," Maynard smiled slyly, "you might say we've kinda struck a friendship. I like her. She's a nice lady. She was real puzzled about how Ella went down so fast. She never even knew Ella was dead."

Later in the evening, Hannah took her book, chair, and bug spray out to the pond where it was cooler. She put her toothpick in place as usual, still a little paranoid about the whole Dimitri thing. She wasn't sorry he'd been caught. He had hurt a lot of people. But he had always been kind to her and Randi, and she thanked him for that.

When the light started fading, she started back to her little townhouse. The toothpick was on the floor. Someone had been here while she was out of sight! She hurried in, shutting the door and locking it. *For all the good that would do*, she grimaced. She sat down for a few minutes of deep breathing before starting a slow, methodical inventory of her belongings. After an hour, she sat down again. Nothing appeared to be missing. Maybe the intruder was just making a dry run for later.

Hannah was spooked. She put the safety chain up and positioned a dining room chair under the door knob. She thought about asking Leon to change her locks tomorrow, but wasn't sure how much she trusted him. He was known to drink a bit, and he might mention it to Rose without thinking anything about it. She finally went into her kitchen to pour a large glass of peach tea. She made it herself, putting sugar in when it was still hot, one of her southern secrets for excellent iced tea. She took the last of what she had and brewed a fresh batch. While the tea was hot, she reached for the sugar canister. Her hand froze.

Hannah's kitchen set had geometrical designs around the edges of the lids. She had become almost compulsive about lining them up just a certain way across all the canisters. The sugar lid was out of alignment. Slowly she took the lid off and set it on the counter. She pulled a large cooking spoon out of the caddy by the stove and stirred through the sugar. Nothing. Next was the large flour canister. Again she stirred, and this time her spoon hit something. She carefully spooned the flour out into a large bowl until she could see the flat object near the bottom. Then she went into her bathroom and pulled a pair of latex gloves out from under the sink. She shook the flour off the object and slid it into a zip-lock bag. When she saw what it was, she almost went into a panic attack. It was Ella Justice's debit card!

Hannah sat on her couch with the card in front of her on the coffee table, trying to keep her mind clear. Someone here knew about her association with Demitri and was trying to frame her. Rose Cassidy said she had given all Ella's Card to that sheriff's detective. That meant that this one was a duplicate. The newspaper articles about Dimitri's arrest said his business had links to Arkansas. Surely not here at Golden Rod Acres. But why not? The pattern for his operatives had been, not only to hack into large data sets, but also to identify rich, vulnerable people and fleece them into poverty. It was easier if you could easily access social security numbers and already had their bank and credit cards to make copies.

Hannah's mind was still running in circles, so she started writing herself notes to help focus her mind:

— Who had access to SS numbers? Rose Cassidy, obviously. The social worker saw lots of forms with SS numbers; even she had occasional access to SS numbers. And, it wouldn't be too hard to go into suites while the residents were out. Hannah wondered if someone had been pilfering personal information while they were at brunch yesterday.
— Who had access to cards? Again, Rose Cassidy. Rose kept cards for residents in the office vault. The vault was new, state of the art with a thumb print scanner and a numbered key pad. Could someone else manage that? It would be a lot of work, but if you were in the office enough, you might get the key pad numbers. And couldn't you get a thumb print from any number of things Rose routinely handled? So, who was in the office a lot? Leon who liked to kibitz and Gracie the social worker. The head cook, too. But her visits were really short. Besides, residents lost and found their cards any day of the week.
— Who would the best targets be? Plenty of money; the self-payers. The lone self-payers. Family would detect missing funds too quickly. A really good thief would take a little at a time from someone who still had control of his/her financial affairs but wasn't paying good attention. And, if there were no heirs, why not continue after death? Ella Justice!

Hannah's mind snapped to attention. There had been very few, no more than one or two, deaths a year since she had arrived four years ago. When people got that sick, they usually were moved to a nursing home. Her patients here had a high probability of heart attacks and strokes, the top killers in the U.S. She racked her brain trying to remember who had died and of what.

Meanwhile, she had somebody on her tail. With any likelihood someone would make an anonymous call to the FBI. Meanwhile she would be in defensive mode. After her evening shower, she used soft bandaging tape to fasten the zip-lock to her body!

32

Sunday evening, Rose Cassidy and Pat Louis were sitting on the balcony of Rose's apartment sipping margaritas. "Did you finish your little chore?" Rose asked.

"Um huh, it was a piece of cake, so to speak," Pat responded. "I put it in her flour canister."

"Good thinking," Rose complimented her. "What better place to hide dough than in the flour? Not that it would do her any good since Hannah's accounts are all frozen."

"That was a piece of luck when Carson told us about Dimitri having an old girlfriend up here. It's like a little bit of insurance. If the Feds come snooping after us, all we have to do is point them at Hannah. By the way, have you heard from Carson since Dimitri was arrested?"

"No," Rose replied, "and I'm a little bit worried. There are some cards that haven't come yet. If the Feds find them they'll be on us like flies, Hannah or no Hannah."

"Well, do you think we should move?" Pat asked.

"Yes and no," Rose equivocated. "I know it's good to keep moving in this business, but we don't have our next location set up. I guess I got a little used to being here. This is the longest we've stayed anywhere for a while. We've got plenty of money to sit tight somewhere. Let's start looking in case we have to leave in a hurry. I rather fancy a lake location, myself."

"Yeah, either that or maybe a beach somewhere. I could become a beach comber for a year or two. Hey, speaking of money, how close is George Tanner to being ready? It'd be a shame to leave before we became his 'beneficiaries'."

"My best guess is by the end of the month at the earliest. We got slowed down because of that ex-wife of his. Maynard is over there every day, and she eats just as much as he does! I heard her complaining about her stomach the other day. Maybe we should just take her out too while we're at it. A double suicide, maybe?"

Pat nodded and smiled. Something to think about.

They continued drinking and talking until they'd had enough tequila to make them sappy. Then they began reminiscing.

"Remember Central Hospital in Omaha?" Pat leaned back in her glider. "That silly little man kept telling me he would report me if I didn't stop flirting with the geriatric patients. I don't know how he thought I was going to pull their information if I didn't. He was just jealous, you know."

"Yes, I think he was. He had no idea what a bad girl you really were. He just wanted you to be bad with him," Rose chuckled.

"Well, borrowing a credit card for one day, then putting it back was good for on-line shopping, but it didn't give us much cash. It was hard to be moderate with all those debit cards sitting there and all those banks within a ten-mile radius."

"I know. I hated that. But you have to hand it to Carson. He knew what he was doing. He told us to take it easy and learn the systems before we got ourselves into trouble. I'll never forget that time I had to put a whole list of card numbers in my mouth because my supervisor came in 15 minutes early!"

Then they moved on to reminisce about St. Louis, their location before coming to Golden Rod Acres. "I really liked St. Louis. The food was better there than in Omaha. Lots of great Italian restaurants. And, we got to start using debit cards. Once we'd stolen the numbers and had Carson make copies for us, all we had to do was sit and wait. Somebody died, and bang! We cleaned accounts before the family knew what had happened."

"I know," Rose agreed, "those were good years. It's just too bad that our friend had to die. I really liked her. Oh well, you got to stay almost a year longer than I did. But, you have to admit the winters are much nicer here."

33

Marshall had so many data requests to get out Monday that he felt overwhelmed. However, some on-the-spot help was available. Marilyn, the departments Administrative Assistant was invaluable. She initiated background checks on all the potential suspects as well as one for Ella. She contacted Golden Rod Acres corporate office in Texarkana and asked for employment records going back the four years since the facility opened. He contacted Dr. Pachebele's office to request death certificates for the people whose names were on the cremains boxes, but substituted Ms. Summermann for Ella Justice. He also asked if the State Nursing Board had a way of contacting Patricia Lewis and whether she was keeping her credentials updated.

He knew it could take up to a week before information began coming in, so he decided to finish his other projects while he had a break. Identity theft in Pope County was often solved in a matter of days. Usually is was somebody who was known to the victim who "borrowed a credit card just until payday". Grandchildren, boyfriends and girlfriends were high on the suspect list. However, there were teams of thieves who went through buildings looking for purses to grab. Beauty salons were often targets of these thieves. Marshall was going out to Walmart this afternoon to look at security footage hoping to find the person(s) who had stolen a courtesy card and proceeded to purchase high dollar gift cards with it.

Then Marshall was going on a scavenger hunt to all the local nursing homes to try to pin down whether any of them was planning to take Ella

Justice in March. Hey, wait, he didn't have to do that. Social workers took care of that in nursing homes. Why wouldn't Gracie have that information? He could call her. Or, he could go out there so he could see her again.

As usual, when he thought he was going to leave, he didn't. The fax in the outer office began turning out copies of death certificates for his five arsenic victims. The first thing that he noticed was that all five had supposedly died of natural causes. And, most importantly, all certificates were signed by none other than Patricia Lewis, RN! It was too strong a pattern to be coincidence.

There was one man, with the others being women; Ella made the sixth death. The deaths had occurred over a four-year period with one in the fall the first year the facility opened, two for years two and three, and one this year. The first death was in late fall; the second, in early spring; then late fall, early spring, late fall. This year brought Ella Justice's death in early spring. Oh, no! Using this pattern, someone else would be expected to die this fall! But when would it be? Ella Justice's gravy train had just dried up. That might accelerate the scam. Man, oh man, he needed to solve this mystery yesterday, already!

He decided to go out to Golden Rod Acres after all, but with a revised plan. He still needed to talk to Gracie, and ask her out for this weekend. And he wanted to talk to the Advanced Practice Nurse who took care of the assisted living residents on a daily basis. But could he trust her? He made a decision to contact his CI. He called Garnet Daniels and left a message. He'd wait a while for her to call. She was probably in a class somewhere. Meanwhile, he'd run by the bank and look at their ATM video.

The video was essentially useless. The dim image of someone with a mustache and a ball cap pulled way down over sun glasses could not be identified, and it couldn't be run through a facial recognition program. Oh, well, he hadn't really expected anything from it anyway. His killer(s) was too savvy to pose for a clean ATM shot.

There was a brief message from Garnet, "the CI says good choice." It was time to take the bull by the horns. He gave his helpers the additional chore of looking through all of Ella's boxes to try to find her donated body forms and any additional financial information. This time he made it out the door.

When Marshall entered the Rec room, there was Maynard playing away at the piano. And there was her wink of recognition. The receptionist was not at her desk, so he started down the hall on his own. He was disappointed when he found a note on Gracie's door saying she was at a funeral and would be back tomorrow. He slipped on down the hall, making a right at the T to go to the nurse's station.

Hannah was at her desk updating and initialing charts. She almost gasped out loud when she looked up to see an officer from the sheriff's office. She felt an adrenalin rush hit her stomach, and her hands felt shaky. She didn't speak, but raised an eyebrow in question. Marshall introduced himself and checked that her name tag was indeed that of Hannah Gibson, APN.

He was very direct. "I need to talk to you confidentially about some residents who died here, including Ella Justice. But I don't think this is the place."

"What kind of information do you need?" she was just as direct, realizing that this might be one way to protect herself from what she believed was coming.

"I need health records from here for these five people," he handed her the list.

She glanced at it briefly then folded it up and slid it into her pocket, nodding slightly to acknowledge that she understood.

'I'm assuming this is not a safe place to meet," he declared quietly. "Can you bring whatever you can find somewhere else?"

She nodded again., looked at her desk calendar, then wrote a time tomorrow and a place on a piece of paper which she slid across her desk to him. He nodded acknowledgement then stood up and left, not stopping to speak to anyone in the hall, hoping no one had seen him, but knowing better.

For her part Hannah thought to herself, *what in the world? This is like something out of a spy movie. It has to be serious since this is his third time out here. Maybe when I pull some records I'll get a hint as to what's going on.* She debated whether to show him Ella's debit card. That decision would have to wait until tomorrow. Meanwhile she had some records to pull.

Hannah spent her afternoon alternating between making her rounds to the residents and pulling old medical files. The hard copy files for the past three years were in storage up at the vault in the shop, while current files for this year were in her office. However, residents' files were backed up on corporate computers to which she had access. She opted to use the computer storage since Leon would undoubtedly report her request to open the storage vault to Rose Cassidy.

It took quite a while to search the archives electronically. There were hundreds of files for each year and some enormous sets of files with information imbedded within. And she felt obligated to shut her programs each time she left her desk. This was not the time to get tripped up by wandering eyes. In addition to medical records, she copied admittance data with personal information. She had a hunch Marshall might want that too, so why go into the archives twice?

That night she took her printouts with her to study at home. Tomorrow morning she would lock them into her car's trunk before coming in to the office. She breathed a sign of relief that the toothpick was still in place. One less distraction tonight!

Hannah took out the five stacks of paper and placed them in a row on her counter. She perused the admission data, looking for similarities, then fixed herself a small ham sandwich and scooped out a serving of the Waldorf salad she had made yesterday. Chopping apples, celery, and nuts had been less therapeutic than she had hoped.

She kept racking her brain, trying to remember these five people. Damn it! She had been here. What had she missed that the detective needed to know? She pulled the medical histories, based on her own recorded data, for each person and laid them out on her coffee table to look at while she ate. She went to the last few pages detailing events about a month before each death.

She remembered Harold Jackson from last fall pretty clearly. He had fallen and twisted his ankle last summer and didn't respond to physical therapy. He was already over weight, but confinement to a wheelchair made it worse. The nurses and aids had moved him out of his suite to the Rec room daily for meals and games, but he claimed he was too weak to do any exercise, and he sat in his suite at night watching TV, eating, and drinking martinis. He was going down fast, and Hannah had recommended to his doctor and Rose Cassidy that he be moved to a nursing home. The move was scheduled to occur while Hannah was on vacation. She had expected him to be gone when she returned, but she hadn't expected him to die!

Janine Waters had died a year ago last spring. She had complained of stomach pains for several weeks before she developed serious vertigo, so much so that she had to use a walker and was afraid to go down the hall by herself. When she came to the Rec room she sat slumped in a chair with her head in her hand, complaining of serious headaches. Hannah remembered her bleary eyes when she asked for more pain killer and took to her bed. She had died last year while Hannah was on her spring vacation during which she took Randi and some friends to Miami.

Little bells ringing. These two, and Ella, had complained of pain and dizziness before taking a serious downturn. And, they had each died while Hannah was out on vacation. Hurriedly, Hannah began flipping through the records for the other three. Sure enough, they followed the same pattern of some form of debilitating pain followed by a rapid downturn and death. And they all died of natural causes, no heart attacks, no strokes, no cancer. And they all died while Hannah was away, and all the death certificates were signed by Pat Lewis!

Oh, no, it can't be, Hanna's mind was processing information. They all died of similar symptoms. And the timing was quite telling. Hannah regularly took off the last week of March and the middle of October to coincide with Randi's school breaks. Most schools in Arkansas had coordinated breaks with their nearest university so faculty, staff, and students were off at the same time. The University of Northeast Oklahoma had the same schedule too. She'd taken these same breaks for four years. Now it appeared that the deaths of six people had been arranged around her vacation schedule!

And the symptoms, what had she missed? Headaches, nausea, vomiting and diarrhea, vertigo, stomach pain, it was as if they had all been poisoned. Lead? Had they all been contaminated with lead? No, not with all new paint and PCV plumbing. Especially not just six. What other heavy metal would give this cluster of symptoms? She picked up her smart phone and Googled heavy metal poisoning. It didn't take her long to come up with arsenic.

34

Midmorning Tuesday, Hannah had an LPN on the staff take over as charge nurse so she could make a short trip into town. She made a point of going by Rose's door to tell her she was going into Russellville to see if Shoe Circus had a special pair of running shoes that Randi wanted. When she got to the store's parking lot, she opened her trunk and carried her tote with her. She was looking at the high-end running shoes when Marshall Boggs came up beside her.

"You don't want those," he informed her. "They don't have enough arch support. You want these," he guided to another group of expensive shoes further down the aisle. "I didn't know you were a runner."

"I'm not. These are for my daughter Randi. She runs cross-country at Talequah, and she never has enough shoes."

"Yep, I know. I ran cross-country in high school. Wasn't very good, but I still wore out lots of pairs of shoes. Is that the info?" he nodded toward her tote.

"Yes, it's all I could find. Is there somewhere we can meet after you've looked at it? I saw some suspicious trends in there. You'll probably see them too."

He looked at his schedule for a minute. "You busy tomorrow night?"
She shook her head.

"OK, I think I have a safe place, but I'll have to check it out. I'll let you know tomorrow."

"How? I'm getting paranoid out there."

'You'll see. There's no way anyone will suspect what we're up to." He picked up the tote and carried it out to his SUV.

The next afternoon, when Maynard knocked at her office door, Hannah looked up and motioned her in. "Miss Hannah, my stomach is hurtin' me somethin' awful," Maynard explained the reason for her visit. She sat down and leaned across the desk closer to Hannah. "Marshall Boggs wants to know if you can come to his friend's for dinner tonight and bring me," she said in a quiet voice.

Hannah's eyes bugged perceptibly, and she started to blurt out something, but Maynard shushed her by putting a finger across her lips. "I'll be at your place at 7:00. We'll take your car. OK?"

Hannah was having trouble getting her mind around this, but she nodded her acceptance.

"My stomach really does hurt, and I've been feeling dizzy too. Can you give me something?

Hannah had Maynard follow her to the nurse's station where she unlocked a cabinet and gave her some Alka Seltzer.

"Is that all?" Maynard whined.

"Yes. And you're lucky to get that, you little pig, eating all that chocolate!"

About five minutes before 7:00, Hannah heard a light tapping at her back door, which faced some woods. She opened it to find Maynard huddled on her little deck, crouched down behind a large planter. Maynard was carrying a limb which she had placed in front of her face, commando style.

"For goodness sakes, get in here," Hannah commanded.

"Turn out the lights," Maynard whispered. Then she hurried through the door.

"What are you doing," Hannah demanded, "playing war games? Aren't you supposed to be wearing cammys and putting black oil on your face?"

Maynard looked as if she had been insulted. "You can't be too careful when you're a CI," she said indignantly.

"A CI?" Hannah took the bait.

"Yes, I'm Detective Boggs' CI, his confidential informant. So there!"

"Well, you're not confidential any more. You just told me," Hannah countered. She wondered just how this had come about, but was afraid to ask.

"That's OK. You needed to know there was someone out here watchin' your back. I know for a fact someone out here is stealin' debit cards. And there's no telling' what else is goin' on."

Hannah opened the door to the tiny garage and proceeded to climb into her Toyota on the driver's side while Maynard crawled into the back seat and hunched down in the floor board. *This is too weird*, Hannah thought, but didn't say anything.

"We're goin' south of Dover on HWY-7," Maynard directed. "I'll tell you where to turn before we get to Russellville." They drove several miles then Maynard popped up in the back, not worried about being seen. "Turn right at the golf course," she instructed, waving a flashlight around to read her directions.

Hannah was becoming less enthusiastic about this little trip when Maynard instructed, "turn into that driveway at the yellow house with white trim." Hannah parked her car next to a vintage Dakota with purple fire. (*Who are these people?*)

Once inside, she recognized several people she had seen before. There was Sheriff Curly McCurly, Detective Boggs, and that woman who had come asking about Ella Justice. What was her name?

"Hello, I'm Garnet Daniels. We met some time ago out at Golden Rod Acres. This is Sheriff McCurly, my husband Mica Manfreid, Tom Wiseman, a local attorney, and you have met Detective Boggs. Gentleman this is Hannah Gibson, and this is Maynard Tanner." They all nodded at the newcomers, and Garnet offered them chairs at the big table beside the kitchen.

When they were all seated with drinks and paper plates for the tray of subs and packages of Cheetos, Sheriff McCurly nodded at Marshall, who took the lead. "We've been workin' on two parallel cases, the murder of Ella Justice, and the theft of her identity." Maynard gasped when she heard the word, murder, but kept quiet otherwise. "Now," continued Marshall, "it looks like we're dealin' with the same person or persons who apparently murdered Ms. Justice to steal her identity."

There was some murmuring around the table. "We start with a set of cremains with names, including Ella Justice's, on the ends of the boxes." He passed out a sheet of paper listing the names. "At approximately the same time, because of a mix-up created by your friends and mine, the Johnny twins, (they all laughed). Ms. Justice's body shows up at the School of Medicine morgue as a donated body under the name Summermann. Dr. Daniels and the other professors recognize the body and begin an investigation.

"Dr. Daniels goes to the Bach Brothers Funeral Home and finds out Ms. Justice's body had been scheduled for cremation, not Ms. Summermann who was a legitimate body donor. However, so was Ms. Justice. So then, why the order for cremation?

"Dr. Daniels then goes to Golden Rod Acres where she questions Nurse Gibson, who tells her that Ms. Justice died of natural causes and that her ashes have been scattered in the Memory Garden. She also reveals that Ms. Justice had no next of kin and no will, which Dr. Daniels knows to be untrue.

"Then Dr. Daniels goes back to the Donated Body records and finds a niece, Scarlett Mars, listed as next of kin. Dr. Daniels contacts plant science departments in several schools, and finally traces Ms. Mars, now Dr. Mars, to UofA. When Dr. Mars learns of her aunt's death, she comes to Russellville to open their shared lockbox and close out Ms. Justice's bank accounts. Lo and behold, the lockbox which allegedly contained a will, the victim's passport, and a piece of heirloom jewelry is empty. And, here is where we pick up the identity theft.

"Dr. Mars has her own copy of the vic's will and contacts Tom Wiseman, who is the will's designated executor. Tom immediately freezes the vic's account and asks for printouts of all activity going back to January of this year. When he gets the printouts, he engages Dr. Freidman to help him decipher the account transactions. They both agree that the account is being drained to the tune of $30 thousand. We'll come back to the money trail later. Right now, Dr. Daniels, fill us in from your side."

"Oh, my, where to start? I knew there was something wrong, but I wasn't sure what. I knew Ella had not been cremated and scattered because her body was in our morgue. My best guess was that the cremains box with her name on it actually held the ashes of Ms. Summermann because of the mix-up. But why hide the boxes unless there was something in those ashes that was incriminating? So, I called Dr. Mars and asked her to request an autopsy based on her being the only survivor plus the evidence of identity theft. Since the body was in our morgue, Dr. Pachebelle did us the courtesy of moving the body to her lab for an autopsy.

"What she found," Garnet continued, "was sobering. Under the nail polish, she found Mee's lines so she took hair samples to look for…"

"Arsenic!" Hannah jumped in. "It was arsenic poisoning! And I didn't catch it. I am so ashamed of myself. I didn't see the pattern until I pulled the old medical records for Detective Boggs. Every one of the people on this list," she waved her piece of paper from the table, "had the symptoms of arsenic poisoning. And their doctors just kept giving them more opioids until they finally quit breathing. That's not really murder is it?"

"Not exactly," Garnet suggested. "Ella didn't die from hydrocodone. She died from an overdose of fentanyl."

"Fentanyl? Where did she get fentanyl?"

"Someone put a patch of fentanyl with 75 or 100 micrograms on her right thigh then removed it before the body was collected. That's why it's murder."

"There's more," Detective Boggs informed them. "How 'bout we take five and stretch a little. Then we'll start back."

"There's more?" Maynard was shaking her head in disbelief.

Garnet opened the back door for some evening air and showed them where the guest half-bath was located. Then she put on a pot of coffee and broke out the chocolate-peanut-butter cookies.

They reassembled and Garnet continued her part of the story. "When Dr. Pachebellee told me arsenic binds strongly to bones, I asked her to test the cremains of the others. She sent me to Detective Boggs to get an official request. And you know the rest. All those cremains tested positive for arsenic except one. Now it looks like the good Detective is searching for one or more serial killers."

"But how do you poison seven people without anyone catching on?" Maynard asked the question for all of them.

"I think I know, at least for Ella and Harold Jackson," Hannah offered. It had to be going in by mouth. And it had to be timed for fall and spring breaks at the universities." They all looked askance at her. "The times of death were coordinated so that I would be gone. They actually appear to have waited for me to go on vacation with my daughter. But, back to the how. Ella had an obsession with chocolate. She had Whitman's Sampler boxes all over the place. She ordered one every time someone went to town. It wouldn't be hard to switch with doctored boxes. Harold was harder. He had just about quit eating, but he was drinking pretty heavy there toward the end. And he loved his martinis. Vermouth! The arsenic was in his vermouth."

"Son of a bitch!" Maynard burst out. "No wonder my stomach hurts. Help! I've been poisoned with arsenic!"

Nobody knew what was going on except Hannah. "I know. I just figured it out last night. George, Maynard's ex, has been ordering a lot of Russel Stover chocolates lately. It seems he and Maynard have been spending some time together, and Maynard, that bad girl, has been eating about half of George's candy. She started complaining a couple of weeks ago, and again, I didn't catch it."

"Oh mercy," Maynard put both her hands up to her face. "It's George. They're after George. He never would write a will, and there's nobody else left in his family. They're gonna kill George!"

"No! No!" Hannah tried to stop her. "They're not. Look, he's just starting to feel sick. He's not nearly as far along as he might be because you've been eating his candy. That's why you're feeling sick. I promise, if you had enough to kill you, you'd be dead. But smaller amounts can gradually build up. That's called sub-acute poisoning. A person can recover from that. Remember the timing. Fall break is in October. My guess is they'll start giving pretty big doses three or four weeks before I leave for vacation."

"But what are we going to do in the mean time. I can't keep eating that stuff. My stomach hurts!"

"I figured that out, too," Hannah was full of ideas. "Someone is dosing the candy then switching the boxes. All we have to do is switch them again. Every time a box comes in, you tell me, and I'll figure out a way to make a switch with a clean box so nobody notices."

The group agreed that Hannah's plan was good. And they admonished her to start checking on the other residents just in case. Since Ella's golden goose had died, they might be in a bigger rush to replace her to keep the gravy train running.

Garnet had another thought, "I think there are at least two people involved. A single person could dose the chocolates and substitute them. But what if the target wakes up when the patch is applied. Wouldn't it make more sense if that person is a nurse who might be just making a bed check? And, who would be there to take the patch off and sign the death certificate?"

"Exactly my thoughts," Detective Boggs chimed in. "I'm tryin' to trace down this Patricia Lewis who comes in when Hannah's gone. It doesn't look right somehow. But then, maybe she's missin' some of the things we've all missed."

It was late so they planned to meet again Friday night. Garnet promised to call Dr. Mars. Maybe she'd be able to join them.

On the way back, Maynard rode up front until they passed the Sonic. Then she had Hannah pull over so she could hide in the back seat. Hannah smiled to herself, allowing the fantasy. Not very many CIs were likely to get this much excitement without being diectly in harm's way.

35

The meeting the next Friday night to begin looking at the financial side of the identity theft of Ella Justice was very informative. Mica and Tom had been analyzing various aspects of the bank accounts, especially now that Marshall had received printouts of the Golden Card Company account from the bank in Ft. Smith.

The Golden Card account was a DBA account with two signatures, Thelma Werner and Irene Watson. Irene Watson died at Golden Rod Acres three years ago. Marshall was still trying to trace Thelma Werner. Checks from two accounts, those of Ella Justice and Irene Watson were being deposited regularly. Ella's checks had stopped just last month when her Russellville account was frozen. Together, the checks added up to $10 thousand a month. Marshall had requested additional printouts for the past four years.

"Well, it's certainly a good thing that Garnet was able to track me down," Scarlett interjected, "or we never would have found this. But where was/is the money going? These monthly statements show most of the balance being written out again."

Mica picked up the narrative, "most of the money went to three different accounts, Master's Art Supplies, Tyson's Printing, and Brevard Shipping. Here is where we run into trouble. Since the Golden Card Company is not in Ella's name, we don't have automatic access to it to find out where they're located. Marshall has issued requests for subpoenas, but we really can't expect anything until next week. I hope we get something before George Tanner dies."

Both Hannah and Maynard laughed out loud. "We've been very bad," Hannah explained. "Rose Cassidy brought in new candy yesterday, and we switched it out, as promised."

"But that's not all," Maynard was beaming. "We took the poisoned box and put it on Rose's desk with a note, FROM A SECRET ADMIRER."

"We did get our background checks," Marshall was obviously pleased. "A friend at the State Police Department walked the requests through for me. Not a lot there. There are no flags on Pat, Rose, or Hannah. Gracie has a sealed juvie record, and Leon drinks a bit. He's had two DUIs in Texarkana, and a citation for possession of a controlled substance (pot)."

"There's not much in the employment records either," Tom reported. "I've been looking at those since Marshall is pretty much swamped. Rose Cassidy has excellent credentials with a strong recommendation from Jewish Hospital in St. Louis. She worked there as office manager for the gastroent… gastroenterology group. I can hardly pronounce it. Rose was hired by corporate.

"Patricia Lewis works mostly as a traveling RN. She's been hard to pin down. The main thing is that she also worked at Jewish Hospital. There's our connection. She was hired by Rose nearly a year after Golden Rod Acres opened.

"Hannah you came here from El Dorado where you were at St. Christopher's. Your references look good. The Medical Director at corporate hired her," he informed the others.

"Gracie came here from Legacy Lodge. I talked with the director there. She said Gracie was really good with elderly people. Hated to lose her." That reminded Marshall that he still needed to check whether a bed had been waiting for Ella Justice.

"Leon," Tom Continued, "was sent up here from Texarkana. He's been at three different retirement facilities. Has a good record with the company in spite of his drinking. He was hired and moved by the Facilities Manager."

"So that's about where we are now," Marshall summed up. We still need those bank reports, and I need to call Jewish Hospital. Maybe they have something. The thing that worries me is that we don't have any real physical evidence to incriminate any of these people. We've got a weak case at best."

Garnet finally spoke, "we'll get something, even if it's just fingerprints on a box of candy. Meanwhile, we need to check to see if anybody else is getting 'special treatment'."

"We've been checking every day," Hannah motioned toward Maynard and herself. "So far nothing noticeable. I have no idea how long this is going to go on. My vacation is usually in October, about six weeks from now. But I bought some spray tan just in case George's skin starts to fade."

Rose Cassidy was heading out to her deck when Pat showed up. Rose poured a second Margarita, and they went out together. "Oh, yummy," Pat saw the big box of chocolates. What's the occasion?"

"I'm not sure. They were on my desk this afternoon with a big red bow. The note said, FROM YOUR SECRET ADMIRER."

"Leon?"

"It might be. He's been buttering me up since I caught him drinking in the shed last week."

"Useless man," Pat was dismissive. "I don't see what corporate sees in him."

"Oh, you know how it is here in Arkansas. He's got to be related to someone."

"Umm," Pat savored a gooey chocolate. "Whoever they're from, they're simply delicious." She closed her eyes in ecstasy as she swallowed, then took another one. "Did we get anything today to put in your lucky safe?"

"No, and I'm getting worried. It's not like Carson to stiff us. This Dimitri thing may have him spooked. At least our cards are not going to be on a list of hacked numbers the FBI found. That's probably a blessing in disguise. The only problem is we're running out of them. We lost almost $6,000 a month when Ella dried up."

"Yeah, what's the use of an identity if it doesn't have any money with it? A passport's not worth much if you're not planning to leave the country. We can't even sell them, not with this Dimitri thing."

36

Carson Kellog was "spooked by this Dimitri thing". He was one of the handful of people who knew where all the bodies were buried. He had been one of the players about 10 years ago. He had recruited and trained any number of identity thieves. And he prided himself on his success. Quite a few of his protégés had never known that Dimitri Popolov was at the top of the pyramid. The deal was simple. His "people" paid him 35% off the top, and he paid Dimitri 30% off the top. There were no broken knees or threats when the agreement was not honored. Suddenly, without warning, the accounts would dry up and the FBI would appear.

With Dimitri out of the picture, at least until he reestablished his kingdom, things were wide open. Everyone had 30-50% more profit. That could buy a lot of muscle, and there were some players who wouldn't hesitate to use it. Identity theft was a lot harder than duplicating cards. It required patience and timing. Timing being the key word. And Carson felt in his gut that it was time to clear out.

Carson's current cover was the Brevard Shipping company in Springdale, Arkansas. His company's specialty was spot shipping and courier services. With so many big companies in the area, his crew never lacked for work. Christmas deliveries alone produced big bucks.

One of the advantages of a shipping company is that it has lots of offices and nooks and crannies where things can be hidden. In the back of his big warehouse, a secret wall hid the $100 thousand of computers and machinery he needed just to duplicate credit and debit cards. Not only that but he fabricated duplicates of just about anything plastic, including lots of fake drivers' licenses and IDs for illegals and underage drinkers. Every time a state or bank card distributor increased the complexity of cards to increase security, Carson had to update his equipment at higher and higher costs.

His back-wall business had dried up two weeks before Dimitri was arrested. That was when he panicked and began destroying his inventory of precut forms. He had kept his own business separate from Dimitri's hackers. Now he destroyed the hard drive on the hacker computer, hoping the proceeds from his own little flock would keep flowing in.

One of Carson's concerns was that someone among Dimitri's numerous clients would give up his name when the FBI came knocking. So, he went into his stash of cleared IDs and picked a new identity for himself. Jackson Freeman had no connection whatsoever with Dimitri or his henchmen.

Carson/Jackson began moving his office and machines. He had previously rented a storage shed for his Bass Tracker on Beaver Lake at Eureka Springs. He packaged his inventory in coolers and plastic storage containers and gradually moved it into the storage space. He had so much stuff that he ended up having to store a lot of it in his boat. Needless to say, there was very little chance of his actually doing any fishing. Never mind, he needed to quit thinking about fishing and get out of Dodge.

When he was sure everything was locked down tight, he drove to Springfield, Missouri, and booked a flight to Little Rock via St. Louis. In Little Rock, he took a taxi to a used car dealer and paid $11 thousand cash for a good used car. Then he headed for Russellville.

Rose and Pat had just moved inside from the deck when Rose's doorbell rang. Rose thought it was the pizza delivery guy and went to the door carrying cash for the pizza and a tip. Pat heard her sharp intake of breath and looked up to see a large man pushing his way into the apartment. She grabbed the tequila bottle to use as a weapon. Then she heard a familiar voice, "Hey, since when do you come to the door with money? I'm not that mercenary." It was Carson Kellog!

37

Carson was a sight for sore eyes. The two women were becoming increasingly paranoid since the news of Dimitri. And having Detective Boggs showing up at Golden Rod Acres every week with more questions about Ella Justice was a bit unnerving. Then there was the loss of $6 thousand of monthly income, a real bummer.

When the pizza arrived a few minutes later, Carson stepped into the bedroom. "Wow, that was a close encounter I just missed. Thankfully, I wasn't coming up the stairs when he arrived. I made sure nobody saw me once I left Little Rock. He took off his hat, thick glasses, and fake mustache. "You got any beer?" he asked Rose as he made himself comfortable.

After the pizza and another couple of beers for Carson, the trio finally got down to business. The first order of business for all of them was Dimitri and his minions. Who knew about Carson's connection, and did anybody know about the two women's connection to Carson?

Carson tried to convince them that his connections to Dimitri were untraceable. "The first thing I did," he explained, "was destroy all that stuff that I did for the hackers. I burned the plastic cards and any hard copy of stolen numbers. And I destroyed, not just deleted, all electronic information about those numbers. You've got to believe that was hard. I really, really, really wanted to keep just a few, just in case. But I knew better.

"It took me almost a week, but I took all my ID equipment and files and hid them. I am out of business for at least three months until things die down. And, I closed my Brevard account and assumed a new identity. Now anyone who is after Carson Kellog for any reason will have to eat dirt. Jackson Freeman truly is a free man!"

"But what about our order?" Pat was quick to ask. "We sent new stuff to you over a month ago. We were worried something had happened you."

"You mean you were worried that if something had happened to me, someone might be on your tail," Carson/Jackson retorted. "Not to worry," he softened the conversation. "I have come with presents." He went back in to the bedroom for his small duffle and opened it. There were the debit cards for several of the patients who "forgot" that they had made purchases last month. And, there was a complete identity package for George Tanner, minus a passport (not George's style). "And, you'll be happy to know that all the monthly fees you sent to Brevard Shipping last week have been hidden away in another account under another alias."

"Oh, well OK," Rose was mollified. "Now what do you think we should do to make sure we're not caught up in Dimitri's mess?"

"You need to forget Ella. We'll do without her money for a while. Destroy anything that can connect her to you or Golden Rod Acres."

Pat looked sheepish, "I hid one of her debit cards in the flour can of one nosey nurse out there, Hannah Gibson. I was going to make an anonymous call to the FBI when the time was right."

Jackson smacked his forehead with an open hand. "Go back and get it. If anyone finds it, you'll have the FBI and local law enforcement snooping around all over the place. You can't afford to draw any attention. You've got to be under the radar on this.

"The next thing you need to do is close all related accounts a.s.a.p. Open new accounts under new names. You do have new names ready don't you?" They both nodded.

"Now, let's talk about the money. You both got money?" They nodded. The truth was that they had been in this business long enough that both had tidy nest eggs stored away. "Tell you what I'll do. Take Ella's contribution... what was that, $6,000 a month? And what is my cut, 35%? That's nearly $2 thousand a month. You keep that for the next three months."

"Why?" they asked in unison.

"Two things," he was very up front with them. "I need your silence. If anybody asks, you have not seen me. Period. And we're all going to need to stick together so we can stay in business. You feed me names, and I feed you cards. It's as simple as that."

They nodded grudgingly. Greed had its limits. "Now, who do you have on deck that we can bring up in three months?"

"Our next "donor" is George Tanner," Rose responded, "old, rich, divorced, no heirs. And he loves chocolate. We started him a couple of weeks ago. We plan to gear up as usual for October".

"Is there any way you can speed him up?"

"We might be able to if we can get Nurse Hannah out of the way for a few days."

"You still got plenty of stuff? I heard the boys in South Dakota got busted for trafficking in fentanyl."

"Yeah, that's right. I've still got about 10 lethal patches of the good stuff. I've already started looking for a new supplier. I have enough odds and ends for a patch for sure. And I should have enough to wring out some patches so we can use a syringe if we don't have time to build up hydrocodone."

Jackson stood up and went in to use the bathroom. When he came out, he picked up his little duffle, said, "it's been good doing business with you, ladies," and walked out the door.

38

The next week crawled by as the Ella Justice case stalled. Marshall was tied up with any number of subpoenas in other counties trying to secure the printouts from the Golden Card Company, then to find the holders of bank accounts the Card Company had sent checks to. There was the Brevard Shipping Company in Springdale (Washington County), Masters' Art Supply (Faulkner County), Tyson's Printing (Pulaski County) and Standard Office Supplies (Washington County). Brevard Shipping had been closed two weeks ago. All the others, plus the Golden Card Company were closed during the week, before any of the account printouts arrived!

Marshall agreed to meet the others at Garnet's Friday night so he would have help working through the financials. That meant that he could take Saturday off. He called Gracie right away to ask her out to dinner and, weather permitting, a drive out to see the Dover lights.

Hannah and Maynard carried out their business as usual with special attention to George. Hannah tasted everything that George ate in his room. He had a little Keurig coffee maker and usually had his last cup of hazelnut cream around 4:00 pm. Maynard changed out all his pods first thing in the morning, and Hannah changed them in the afternoon. They found one that had a white powder in it, but couldn't be sure it wasn't the cream in the hazelnut mixture. Hannah was concerned that George didn't seem to be getting any better. It was almost as if the chocolate had never been switched. She began to look for another source of arsenic in his daily routine.

The two of them put more effort into the chocolate exchange this week. Hannah stopped at Dollar General and bought a Thinking of You card and a big blue bow. The message was the same, FROM YOUR SECRET ADMIRER. Maynard stood guard while Hannah placed the candy on Rose's desk. She sat playing the piano with "Take me Out to the Ball Game" as the designated signal.

Rose and Pat were the busiest ones. They had to drive to all their banks to close accounts. Pat took Bentonville, and Springdale in the Western part of the state. Rose took Conway and Little Rock. The two agreed to hold the cashier's checks several weeks until they could take an afternoon together to open a Bronze Card Company in Hot Springs.

Rose began looking for conferences and workshops to send Hannah to. Hannah needed yearly continuing education credits to retain her registration, so she did take professional leave for a day or two throughout the year. Many of the workshops were on weekends, so she had a good bit of comp-time built up. Rose was reluctant to do the fentanyl dosing on a weekend when lots of extra people were likely to be around, so she kept looking for a midweek venue.

Meanwhile Pat had to sneak around to be sure that Hannah would be away from her house for a while so she could remove the possibly incriminating card. She used Rose's master key at 1:00, the beginning of the Hannah's afternoon nursing rounds to let herself in. She went straight to the flour canister and dug down into it with a spoon she found in the sink. Nothing! She dug again. Exasperated, she found a bowl and dumped the whole canister into it. Nothing! Now she was scared as she cleaned up her mess and hurried out the back door. Where was it? Who had it? Did she leave any fingerprints on it? Oh my!

Garnet caught up on her lecture prep, lab quizzes and grading. She tried to get a little ahead so that she could free up time if she were needed on Ella's case. She even had time for the Thursday lady's lunch with her colleagues. After chit chat about personal activities and an accounting of all the pets, the conversation turned to anatomy. Each of the ladies had had one or more anatomy courses, and some of their experiences were worth telling. Rachel Pachebelle told about her first undergraduate anatomy course. They were learning the bones and their markings, and the guy next to her at the table was having a really hard time visualizing how the *os coxae* (hip bones) fit together. He kept turning them the wrong way and nothing was fitting. The instructor came by and showed him how they articulated, with the pubic bones fused together toward the front and pointed out that the *pubic synthesis* was just that, the bones that lay under the pubic area. "So this guy," Rachel went on, "sticks his hands down the front of his pants and feels around and says, 'oh, yes, they do!' I was totally freaked out," Rachel laughed. "I grabbed my books and said, 'I think I'd better go to my next class.'"

"Do you remember dirty mnemonics?" Garnet asked. "I was really shocked when the instructor told us how to remember the cranial nerves: oh, oh, oh, to touch and feel a girl's vagina and hymen (or a guy's vas and hiney)."

"We had a male and a female cadaver for the entire class," Hattie West picked up the conversation. "The TAs were responsible for the prosections (dissections done before the students see the materials). One of the guys, Art, was dissecting the male genitals when he made a kind of choking sound. The rest of us gathered around to see what the problem was. This cadaver had a penile implant in one side. It was a soft, resin thing in the exact shape as the *corpus spongiosum*. None of us had ever seen one, so it was quite the find. We teased Art by referring to it as the 'artifact'."

Tom and Mica took the week off from their financial analysis. They had plenty of work to do on other projects. Ella's bank had begun its own investigation of bank fraud. Since bankers often could get information faster than the sheriff could via the subpoena process, there was a real chance for a breakthrough on the identity of the various account holders who benefited from deposits from the Golden Card Company.

39

Friday night was a useful meeting. Just like last week, Maynard showed up at Hannah's back door then hid in the backseat of the car. One important difference was that this time she brought her famous lava cake. Garnet set out cheese and fruit, and Mica picked up chicken spaghetti from Mary's Kitchen. They savored Maynard's runny chocolate cake bite by bite as they began the business at hand.

Subpoenas for all available information about the fraudulent accounts had resulted in a large pile of printouts that had arrived after 3:00 pm on that very Friday. Mica and Tom had their charts from last week showing the four accounts used to launder the money going out of the Golden Card Company. Now they wrote the names of the account holders under each bank account. Besides the Golden Card Company held by Thelma Werner and Irene Watson, Masters Art Supplies in Conway was held by Harold Jackson and Ella Justice; Tyson's Printing in Little Rock, by Estelle Painter and Lelani Kelley; Standard Office Supplies in Benton, by Opal Watson and Ginger Arnold. And Brevard Shipping was held by Pierre Brevard, or whoever he was. Of these, Janine Waters, Irene Watson, Estelle Painter, Harold Jackson and Ginger Arnold were names on the death certificates matching the boxes of cremains Uncle ADD had dug up. All had died while at Golden Rod Acres.

"Wow, that's impressive!" Marshall exclaimed. "Identity theft and serial murder! Or, serial murder to steal identities."

"Um huh," Tom agreed. "We know about the folks from Golden Rod Acres. But who are Thelma Werner, Lelani Kelly, and Ginger Arnold?"

"I'm afraid to ask because I think I already know the answer," Marshall replied. I'll have Dr. Pachebelle check for death certificates. But these three could be from almost any state. Our ladies came here from St. Louis, so Missouri is the next best place to try. And, speaking of death certificates, my assistant at the office managed to track down all the accounts from Golden Rod Acres and get death certificates to the banks. Our thieves will not get another penny from those accounts!"

"I know I said I couldn't do any more analysis without more information," Mica announced, "but I lied. I looked at the pattern of deposits into the Golden Card Company. Last year six of our victims were making monthly deposits to total a little over $6 thousand. This year Harold Jackson and Ginger Arnold dropped out. Janine Waters also dropped out, leaving three people still in the pool, Estelle Painter, Irene Watson, and Ella Justice, making deposits totaling over $13 thousand a month, that is, until Ella dropped out too. Based on Ella's pattern, there should have been cash withdrawals from all of them. Quite likely the nearer the bank is to us, the more cash withdrawn. Driving to Little Rock or Springdale every week to pull out a limited amount of cash could get to be a real pain.

"My point in all this is that the monthly checks we see here were being written from three accounts. Ella replaced one of the drop-outs, probably an account frozen when a relative finally showed up, and a fourth victim would be expected this fall. Once Ella's accounts had been frozen, our thieves were down to two rather slim accounts. And now, those two have been frozen. I predict they'll move quickly to restore their take."

"There's one thing that's been bugging me," Garnet looked perplexed. "Why a male victim? Harold Jackson dropped out; now George Tanner has been moved up. Why a man? We've been assuming that we're dealing with women. Why a male identity?"

"I see your point," Marshall agreed. He turned to Hannah and Maynard, "is anyone else besides George getting special attention?"

Maynard shrugged her shoulders, but Hannah seemed perplexed. "There is one other possibility. (I could shoot myself for not catching it earlier.) Lettie Bronfels has been complaining about stomach pain, but since she's not on the chocolate train, it took me a while. But, she's a sherry drinker. Alcohol, chocolate and caffeine are the three most common foods that upset GI tracts. I guess I'd better start looking at my coffee slurpers too. There are quite a few of those in that age group."

Then another possibility occurred to her. "Maynard, George doesn't drink any more does he?"

"No way!" Maynard was emphatic. "He quit a good ten years ago now. I keep askin', and he keeps swearin' that he's still on the wagon. I'm there every day now, so I don't see how he could sneak any liquor in."

After a brief pause, Maynard made a good suggestion. "We'd better get Lettie some clean sherry just like we got George some clean chocolate. I can always make an excuse to go out to Blackwell. I call it solution 101." Pope County is a dry county with private club licenses, but no package stores. So those evil people who choose to drink liquor must drive the 20 miles to Blackwell where two liquor stores are parked just past the line into Conway county at Exit 101.

"OK, who wants to make the run to Blackwell?" Garnet asked. "I really don't need anything right now. I still have two boxes of Real Sangria, but I'll go if need be."

"I'd better check to see which brand Lettie drinks," Hannah hedged. "I really don't know. I'd hate for us to get the wrong kind. Let me check first thing in the morning."

"It's a deal," Garnet agreed. "You let Maynard know, and Maynard can call me. Anyone else want something since I'm going?"

"Another thing," Marshall held up his index finger for emphasis, "we need her current bottle to test for arsenic. It could be important supporting evidence. The thing that really rubs me about this case is that almost all our evidence is still circumstantial. I'd like to get something more concrete. Even if her sherry has arsenic in it, any number of people could have laced it."

40

Marshall was looking forward to his Saturday date with Gracie, even though there was still the matter of whether Ella had a bed waiting in a nursing home when she died. He'd have to think up some clever way to worm the information out of Gracie without signaling his intentions.

He picked her up just a little before dark, and they headed up HWY-7 to Cliff House for an early supper. They chatted along the way about where they each had been and how they got to this place. Marshall, like many less affluent blacks had joined the Army straight out of high school. The boot camp discipline had scared him, mostly because he was used to speaking his mind, and he realized how easy it would be to get booted out.

He was placed in communications and was deployed to Afghanistan where he usually stayed behind the fire line as a radio operator. He had taken advantage of educational opportunities and had finished almost 90 hours of college before he left the service. Then he completed the police academy training in Little Rock and joined the police force. It took him three more years to finish a degree in Criminal Justice while he was on the force.

"What headed you toward Little Rock?" she asked.

"I'm a Louisiana boy, born and raised in Monroe. But I do have some relatives in Arkansas. So when one of my Army buddies mentioned that there were law enforcement jobs waitin' in Little Rock, I decided to give it a try. My mother is really old fashioned. You don't go any where you don't have folks. But since her cousin Alberta and her family live there, she was all right with it."

"How'd you get to be a detective?" she asked the obvious question.

"After the academy, I worked patrol two years and started taking more classes towards a criminal justice degree. You probably know Little Rock was losin' officers faster than they were replacin' them. Two detectives took higher payin' jobs up north. I applied for a position and was accepted for a six-month trial. Surprisingly, a lot of guys didn't apply because of the erratic hours, but that's one of the things I like about being a detective."

"What are some of the things you detected?" she was curious.

"Theft and theft by receivin' made up the bulk of my cases. Children taken by the non-custodial parent popped up from time to time, and you'd be surprised how many dogs are kidnapped to be sold. Mutts are a lot safer in the back yard than registered pups.

"They wanted me to go into homicide, but I got to see enough bodies in Afghanistan. Little Rock has a big enough underclass that murder is no big deal for lots of folks. I never understood how you could just close your mind off and shoot somebody for no real reason at all."

"What about Russellville?" she asked. "How did you get this job?"

"Oh, that was a bit of a fluke. My supervisor knew somebody else's supervisor who said the Sheriff's Department needed an experienced detective, and I was recommended. You should have seen their faces when a black man showed up for the interview. I guess they decided to buck the tide because about a week later I got an offer. They did try to low ball me on salary, but they really needed a 'more diverse' department, so I got what was fair. I mean, how many black men with a college degree and detective experience were they going to get?" he laughed at the memory.

"Do they treat you right?"

"I'd have to say yes, most of the time. There are a couple of guys who come on all hostile, but it takes time. You have to work with a lot of people before you figure out that you need the good guys out there. The bad guys are all the same. The only thing they see is you standin' between them and what they want. And believe you me, they'll take you out if they get a chance. Sometimes it gets really hard to work where the only thing you see is the underbelly of your town. Then you look around and see the people who need you. They'll hide because they're scared, but they're on your side when the rubber meets the road."

"Yeah, I think the people here are really nice, she agreed. They're always trying to help each other. There's not a lot of money, but that doesn't keep folks from having a fund raiser. There must be two or three every week. And when someone gets sick, they go visit them in the hospital, and in nursing homes. I've seen people who are in worse shape than the person they're visiting.

"Nursing homes aren't nearly as scary as they used to be. I found lots of times it was the families who freaked out about putting someone in a nursing home, not the patient. I guess they feel guilty. There's a strong sense of family here in the River Valley, and you're supposed to keep your family at home. But that's not the way it works out. It doesn't mean you don't love people. It just means that you've accepted the truth that you just can't do it. That's the hardest thing in the world for lots of folks."

They had open-faced beef sandwiches with green beans and cole slaw and iced tea. They shared a giant piece of peanut butter cream pie for dessert. He switched to black coffee, but she stayed with tea. They picked up their conversation with her time at nursing homes.

"Tell me why you decided to work at nursing homes," he prompted.

"Well, I started out in counseling. I thought maybe I'd work at a school somewhere while I took more classes to get my family certification. But then my grandma got sick. She was the one who practically raised me. My mom was there too, but she was always working, supporting me and Grams. And," she hesitated, "she was gone a lot. She liked men, and she liked to party, so Grams and I spent most evenings together.

"We were doing fine until my junior year at MNSU when she had a stroke. At first, she just stayed in bed or sat and watched TV. Then I think she probably had some more mini-strokes. I got home after class one night and found her on the floor. I called an ambulance and they took her to St. Mary's. She never did get any better, really. So they found her a bed at Legacy Heights.

"If you go from the hospital to a nursing home, Medicare pays for 120 days. I panicked when it became obvious Grams was going to need long-term care. We didn't have any money. That's when I learned how important a good social worker is. Miss Marian sat me down and went through all the finances with me and helped me fill out all the forms for Grams to get Medicaid. I was real embarrassed about not being able to pay for my own grandmother, but

Miss Marian told me a little secret about how 80% of Arkansans in nursing homes are on Medicaid."

When she looked as if she were going to tear up he reached across the table to take her hand.

"I'm all right," she smiled. "I loved that old woman something awful, and finding a way to get her taken care of meant all the world to me. Anyway, I was looking at graduate programs for psychology certification when I realized with a few extra classes I could get a sociology degree. That and 25 cents lets you sit down at the welfare office and take applications for food stamps."

"But you went on, didn't you?" he asked rhetorically.

"Yeah, I took a night job at the hospital processing Medicare and Medicaid forms for the Billing Department. Then I moved to days and was an assistant to one of the social workers. Those two jobs together taught me so much! I could have moved to intake, but I was more interested in where the patients went than where they came from."

Marshall glanced at his watch. It was early, but getting dark. He paid the bill and they started back down the road to try to find the Dover lights.

41

A good viewing place for the Lights of Dover was located west of HWY-7 about 10 miles northwest of Dover on Old HWY-7. Marshall used his GPS to locate the spot. He turned right onto NFR- (National Forest Road) 1801, also known as Old Highway Seven. Then he turned right onto Maupin Flat Road (or Treat Road) and on to the viewing site about two miles further.

A short rock wall separated the edge of the old road from the sharp incline into the trees. The approximately 40 feet of 30" tall by 20" wide sandstone wall had been built during the Depression by CCS workers. It was probably once a guardrail and still served that function for people who came to look for the lights. Marshall positioned two comfortable folding chairs side by side at about the middle of the wall.

"Where are the lights?" Gracie wanted to know. "When people said they were north of Dover, I thought they'd be just out of town."

"I'm not your best reference for this," Marshall admitted. "This is my first time here too. The lights are supposed to be along that ridge way over on the opposite side of the Piney."

"You mean there's water down there?"

"Oh, yeah. This road would have been built along the ridges beside the river. Then it was straightened out later," he laughed. The idea that Scenic-7 was straight was comical. It was the kind of road you wanted to drive in a sports car. One of the scariest things that could happen was to drive around a blind curve only to find yourself facing an 18-wheeler barreling along over the speed limit right in the middle of the road. By the time you had your flash of adrenalin and instant vision of a head-on crash, the driver of the truck would have his rig back over on his side heading for the curve you had just come around.

It was a clear night, perfect for viewing. The moon was just beginning to stick its head over the horizon. "Is there going to be enough light?" Gracie queried.

"It should be just about right tonight. The moon will be full next week, and too much light makes pale lights harder to see."

"What kind of lights are we looking for?"

"I don't know, but I've been told that any color of light can show up over there on the ridge. But most people see a white light shaped kind of like a ghost about half-way down the ridge. I really don't know what to expect."

As they sat waiting for the lights to show themselves, several cars of light seekers pulled into the area to join them. The other parties had probably come out mainly to smoke pot or drink moonshine. When they saw the van with the Pope County Sheriff logo, they stayed a short while then left.

After over an hour of waiting, Gracie pointed to the opposite ridge. "There," she exclaimed, pointing to a spot about half way down the ridge. "There's something white, and it's moving!"

Marshall saw it too. To him it looked ghostly, but more like a cartoon ghost than a person. "Yeah," he agreed, "I see it too." The light was there for no more than 10-15 seconds before disappearing.

"What causes the lights?" Gracie wanted to know.

"Well, there are lots of explanations. Some say it's Indian spirits. The Cherokee and Osage Indians would have hunted on the river. Some say its coal miners who were trapped when a mine collapsed. Or, there might have been a hidden silver mine up there, and people who lived over 100 years ago are still hunting for it. Your guess is as good as mine."

They watched another half hour without seeing anything, so they decided to pack it in. Marshall was putting his little cooler in the SUV when the moonlight hit Gracie just right. He saw motion behind her left foot. "Freeze!" he shouted at her. "Don't move your feet. There may be a snake behind you!"

At the word, snake, she did freeze, closing her eyes and hoping it would slither by. Instead she felt a light tickle on her left ankle. Curious, she braved a downward look. A little ball of dark fuzz was sniffing around her ankle.

Marshall came quietly up on the other side of the van with his lantern. It was a baby skunk! When he searched with his LED beam, he picked up more movement. A mother skunk with a beautiful plume of a tail was snarfing up little pieces of potato chips someone had left in the dirt.

"Just be patient," he cautioned Gracie in a very quiet voice. "They'll move on when she finishes her snack. If you keep still around skunks, you don't usually get sprayed."

"Usually?" Gracie was not comforted by his optimism. She was the one who had almost stepped backwards onto the baby skunk.

The skunk family did move on, and Gracie and Marshall loaded the rest of their chairs and gear, but not before he put his arms around her to stop her shaking. "You all right?" he asked.

She took a deep breath before replying, "I know people come up here and never see any lights, but I doubt any of them ever got literally skunked."

42

As the dark of the moon passed and the new moon waxed, Beulah Lamb began meeting people in her dreams again. Being a yellow dog Republican, she was leery of important Democrats. Just couldn't trust those rascals. Beulah was floating through the halls of congress when she encountered Rep. Nancy Pelosi, of all people. She would rather have met Sen. Tom Cotton, but this was, after all, just a dream.

Nancy was impeccably dressed in a red wool suit with pearl earrings and a gold watch. As far as Beulah could see, Nancy's biggest problem was her six inch heels. Her legs were too sort for her to have a smooth stride, and she pitched forward noticeably at the waist. All in all, Beulah was impressed by how good Pelosi looked. "You'd look good too if you'd had as many face lifts as she has," a voice came from off to the side. It was Maxine Waters the representative from California. "I swear that woman has had too many face lifts."

"And you haven't had enough," Pelosi snarked back at the saggy-faced Waters.

"But you're not dead," Beulah interjected. "Most of the people I dream about are dead."

"Oh, she's dead all right," Maxine opined. "Dead in the water. She used to be Speaker of the House, toady to Harry Reid. Now look at her. Her career is over, I tell you. She's dead, dead, dead."

"You're just jealous because you're not minority leader in the House,"

Nancy rejoined. "You thought just because you're a diva in the Black Caucus, everyone should kowtow to you. If you think my career is dead, your's never started. You just don't have leadership potential."

"Oh, yeah, just look who's talking. You'll be lucky if you get elected again. Do you really think they're going to keep you around until the Democrats retake Congress just so you can be Speaker again? How many more face lifts is that going to take?"

Beulah left the quarreling women and floated down the halls observing any number of closed-door conversations. She was particularly concerned that all the restrooms were marked, Men. She searched and searched for a woman's restroom to no avail and woke up with a dangerously full bladder. She told herself it was just another "potty dream". In her dreams she often found herself seeking out nonexistent, or out-of-order toilets when her bladder was full.

As the full moon approached, Beulah began having dreams about a truly dead person, Orville Faubus. She would rather have talked to Roy Rogers, but these people just showed up. It wasn't as if they were invited. "Little Rock, Little Rock, Little Rock," Faubus ranted. "Look at all the things I did for Arkansas, and what do I get remembered for? Little Rock!"

Beulah would just as soon not have this conversation. She knew that people outside Arkansas thought they were all racists. She wanted to tell them about Hoxie and Charleston and other small towns that were open to integration. And she wanted to tell them about Faubus' home county where they always had been integrated because it made no sense to pay for separate facilities for one black family. She toured the halls of Central High School looking for a restroom. They were all marked "blacks only". She woke up with a full bladder again.

Faubus kept infiltrating her dreams. She wanted to send him away, but the man had a very high opinion of himself and refused to go. Finally, in the days just before the full moon, he stated his business, "you need to go to the Zion Lutheran Cemetery at Augsburg. There's something up there that goes with the treasure you got from Jesse James."

"How did you know about Jesse James? These are my dreams, not yours."

"Well, let's just say that us outlaw heroes have a way of talking to each other. Go to the old part of the cemetery. Look over by the woods. You'll find something very interesting."

"Did you put it there?"

"No I did not." Then he repeated, "look over by the woods. You'll find something very interesting."

Beulah didn't know how to approach Uncle ADD. He was still disgruntled that she had led them to dead people's bones. When she told him about her dreams, not the one about Pelosi and Waters, he was very dismissive. "No, now, we're not goin' up there. Faubus ruined our reputation for us. I'll not give him a chance to ruin something else!" he was most emphatic. Besides, what does 'over by the woods' mean? Were you expecting a big sign saying 'Dig Here'?"

"Now, Addie, there's no reason to get upset. It's just a few dreams. But I am a little curious. Do you think we could find it with the moonstone?"

ADD's eyes bugged out. "Moonstone? How did you know I had the moonstone? Are you spyin' on me, Woman?"

"Now, Addie," she started again. "You told me that night you knew where you threw it. Since Raymond still hasn't come around, I just figured you went out there and got it so you could see for yourself if it was really evil."

"Well, nothing bad has happened since I brought it back in and put it in its little sack. So I reckon it's not really evil like Raymond says. But I can't use it. I'm not the seventh son of a seventh son, you know."

"He isn't either," she rebutted him. "You're a good, righteous man, and you have just as much right to that stone as Raymond Bailey who is entirely too superstitious for my liking."

"Well, when you look at it that way," ADD had been looking for an excuse to use the stone. He really wanted to find out if it would work for him. "I suppose it wouldn't hurt to give it a try. The worst we can do is come up with nothin'. When's the next full moon?"

43

Saturday was business as usual. When Garnet delivered the sherry, Hannah managed to slip into Lettie Bronfels' room while Lettie was playing bingo. She slipped on a pair of latex gloves and picked up the bottle of Taylor's Cream Sherry. She held it up to the light to try to gauge the volume through the dark glass. Then she eased it into an evidence bag that Marshall had given her Friday night. She poured almost half of the sherry from the new bottle into the toilet and flushed it twice. Now she was sure Lettie had a non-doctored bottle, and when this bottle was gone, there'd be another clean bottle waiting.

Sunday, Hannah passed the bottle of sherry to the CI so Maynard could deliver it Monday morning. Then she drove to Muskogee to meet Randi for supper and to clear her mind that was understandably uneasy about the danger that was developing at Golden Rod Acres.

The oppressive heat of August was easing a little bit as the days of September shortened bit by bit. Sunday evening, Pat invited Rose to go with her for a short drive before dark. Rose was still having stomach troubles and declined. Pat had advised her to lay off those chocolates, but they kept calling Rose, "come get me; come get me." Rose was more worried about what weight she might be gaining than her achy stomach. She'd even given up her Margaritas in favor of those yummy chocolates, all the time wondering who her secret admirer could be.

Pat headed her old Toyota north of Russellville. She had considered driving down to the Galley Rock Cemetery, but since the days were shortening, she opted for the Zion (Augsburg) Cemetery. Pat loved those old cemeteries dating back to the 1800s. It was more than a sense of history. It was almost a sense of family.

Like her victims, Pat had very few relatives, and they most certainly were not in her future plans. The thought of leaving something in a will made her laugh. What name would she use? What were the names of her real relatives? The whole idea was ludicrous.

Pat drove along side the Lutheran church with its back to the cemetery. Like Galley Rock, the burials had begun in the 19th century, but this community was different. These were not merchants and traders. These were German farmers. And unlike Galley Rock this community had survived.

Germans from the Midwest came to this area in the 1880s. Many bought land from the Iron Mountain Railway Company. They were joined in the community of Augsburg by their Lutheran religion and were known to have worshiped in an open field before building a small church that was dedicated in 1883.

A new building in 1907 was known for its gigantic bell that rang out the beginning of the Sabbath and the times of worship. When the bell tolled out a sad, sad sound during the week, the community knew someone had died. That building had burned in December of 1978, and the bell fell and broke. Bowed, but not broken, the Augsburg community built a third church in 1979. Dedication was in 1980.

Pat was quite taken by Augsburg's story. She was fascinated by the wedding traditions. Even though she had never been married, she could imagine herself walking down the aisle with her future husband and reciting simple vows. She would be dressed in a brightly colored blue dress with doves of peace embroidered on the bodice and soaring birds festooning the skirt.

Tonight, Pat visited the Zion Lutheran Cemetery. The old German names on the stones reminded her of her own German people from southern Indiana. The German words, *Geliebt Mutter und Grossmutter* (Beloved Mother and Grandmother) brought back memories of her own family. She didn't have to wonder what her mother and grandmother would think of her now. They would be horrified. Man was to live from the sweat of his brow, not from someone else's labor.

Pat was fascinated by old cemeteries where she experienced a connection to people long past. Sometimes as she stood by an old, old marker, she could feel herself reaching into the past and connecting with the dead in a way she was never able to connect with the people around her. She had wrapped herself in the lore of Galley Rock, and had taken the boxes of cremains there so that those souls could be enveloped in the timelessness of death.

Tonight, she wandered amid the tombstones until she came to the back of the cemetery where the oldest bodies lay quietly in death. She approached the stone of Greta Baughman and knelt to place a small vase of artificial flowers that she carried with her each time she visited. She felt connected to this grave and to this person who, in another time, could have been part of her very own family.

Pat had grown up in a middle class family in southern Indiana. There were lots of German families there where farming was good. Pat's family had been moderately loving and supportive, nothing to really complain about. But her German friends, like Trudy Steuben had close families that gathered as a community around their church and relatives. Pat attended some of their functions and secretly wished her parents were German. That was when Pat constructed her own German family in her mind with ancestors traceable back to the time of immigration in the early 1800s.

Surprisingly, when Pat met Trudy Steuben at a university function some years later, Trudy wasn't Trudy. She was Arlene. And when she met her about a year later, Trudy was Judith. What was going on? Trudy confided in her that it was easy to change your identity if you had the right information.

Pat never had so much fun as when she was changing identities. Then Trudy taught her how to make extra money with the stolen identities. Then Trudy introduced her to Chuck Iverness who later became Carson Kellog. From Indiana to Illinois, to Missouri, to Arkansas, the friends kept changing identities, and they kept moving. Whenever Pat was feeling guilty about their latest theft, she returned to the identity of Pat Lewis, little girl from Indiana who wanted to be German.

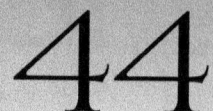

When Pat got back to her apartment, there was a message from Rose, "hey, something came up while you were gone. Come on over so we can talk." Pat would rather have spent the evening alone, reminiscing about life in general, and her own specifically, but she laid out her underwear and uniform for tomorrow's assignment then crossed the building to Rose's.

What had "come up" was Carson Kellog. "Hi there, Pat," he waved lazily from his comfortable position on the lounge. "Thought I'd just drop in and visit my favorite girls."

"Carson's got a problem." Rose cut right to the chase. "The FBI is looking for Pierre Brevard, and he needs a place to crash."

"And?" Pat knew the two of them had already made a plan. They'd ask if she had any ideas, but her input didn't matter at this point.

"Well, here's the thing," Carson explained. "They'll know by now that I've already left Springdale, and if they're any good, they'll have tracked Carson Kellog to St. Louis, and maybe Little Rock. But there's no reason for them to look for me here. Especially since Carson will have disappeared, and they don't know about Charles Ballard, my new identity."

"I thought you were Jackson Freeman," Pat interjected.

"You can't be too careful," he responded.

"I assume you have plenty of money?" Pat asked. When he nodded, she continued. "Where are you planning to stay?"

"Right here with you two," he announced. "Pat, I'll need to stay with you a couple of days until my new living arrangements can be finalized."

"So you have a place?" Pat needed more information.

"This is the good part," Rose interjected. "There just happens to be an opening in Assisted Care at Golden Rod Acres!"

"Isn't there a waiting list?" Pat didn't want Rose to get caught putting someone ahead in line. That kind of thing could cause an eruption that could be heard all the way to Russellville.

"Of course there's a waiting list. But we never tell anybody when they'll come up. I don't even tell my assistant. Too much blabbing between relatives around here."

"And when is Mr. Ballard moving in?"

"Tuesday, if we can get the paperwork done. Can you bring him in tomorrow? He can't drive himself if he needs to be in assisted living."

"And what does he need assistance with?" Pat was skeptical.

"He has an inner ear problem and falls a lot. Show her," Rose instructed Carson/Charles.

Carson managed to get up from the lounge, but staggered and grabbed one arm to keep from falling. He headed for the bathroom, but grabbed on to furniture along the way and ended up weaving around the door frame. "I'm going to need a walker for sure," he commented as he closed the door.

Pat looked at Rose in amazement. "Do you really think this will work?"

"I think it's brilliant," Rose crowed. "We'll have to cut his hair, but the beard is perfect. You can go out tomorrow to get him some new used clothes. There are several good thrift shops around the downtown area. I'll make you up a list so he'll fit right in out there."

When Carson/Charles came back from the bathroom, the three talked seriously about the risks involved in their plan. They all agreed that this could be one of their best scams yet.

One of the first things they settled was what to call their new man. Rose and Pat had known him as Carson for about eight years. Charles was a little too formal for both of them, and Charlie was Rose's brother's name. They finally settled on Charles in public and CC in private.

It was almost midnight when the talking wound down and Pat stood up. To her surprise CC got up too, snagged his duffle, and followed her to the door. "You're coming with me?" she was surprised.

"Yeah. I figure you're not as well known as Rose, so I'd be better off hiding out with you. And you have to take me out to see my new residence and buy me clothes. This will be more convenient for all of us. Night, Rose." Rose looked slightly annoyed. She and CC had been an item back in St. Louis. Admittedly the fire had died long ago, but a girl could hope. That's what fantasies are for.

As soon as the deadbolt was turned on Pat's door, CC moved in for a big hug and a kiss that started as a peck then became quite firm with a little tongue. Pat kissed him back then asked, "What about Rose?"

"Don't worry about Rose. She'll get to see plenty of me once I move in out there. You're the one I'm thinking of now. It's been too long. How about a shower and bed?"

45

While CC and Pat were rolling around in bed and planning their day, Marshall was on the job. He put on a call to Personnel at Jewish Hospital in St. Louis. A Ms. Sue Kochner answered his questions, but was not much help. She had been there only two years and had not known either Rose Cassidy or Pat Lewis. And, it would take two to three days to pull up their employment files because the hospital had changed its filing software last year, and the older files had been switched only for current employees. The older files still existed and had been archived, but they had been processed on a different platform. So those files would have to go to computer services to be translated to the new format, and that would take a couple of days

Is this the run around or what? Marshall thought to himself. But he agreed to let Ms. Kochner request the files and get the process started. She also said she'd ask some of the older employees if they remembered the two women. He made a phone appointment with her for Thursday morning.

Just before noon his CI made a stealthy entry into his office and closed the door. Maynard had brought the cream sherry bottle for analysis. Marshall completed the paperwork and sent the dark bottle over to the State Crime Lab for Hattie West or one of her minions to test for arsenic.

Pat and CC had plenty of time to shop for his new image before their 2:00 appointment at Golden Rod Acres. Before they left the apartment, Pat gave CC a haircut more in line with that of an older man since his hair wasn't quite long enough for the ubiquitous ponytail the old hippies around here were wearing.

The first place they went was Marva where they picked up some practically new shirts and even found one with the tags still on it. Their grand find was a gently used walker to help CC with his balance. They decided his shoes would be fine then spent quite a bit of time looking for frames that he could slip his lenses into. His designer glasses were a bit toney for his new look.

Pat stopped at the drive-through at Arbys for gyros, and they went back to her apartment to wash and dry CC's new clothes. After he had fiddled with his glasses long enough to switch the lenses, he tried out the walker. The back legs kept dragging on the carpet, and he really did look off balance when he changed directions. Pat changed her appearance with a grayed wig and outdated glasses with clear lenses plus a heavy application of lipstick. Then they were off to meet Rose.

The interview went very well as each of the players stayed in character. Rose explained the rules and limitations and showed the couple around the facility. CC's room was over on the east wing between two other men. Its latest occupant had just moved out last Friday, and house keeping would need another day to get the room ready. It was identical to the other rooms with a small living room and kitchen area. There was no stove. A microwave was allowed, but cooking was strongly discouraged, hence the tiny sink and office size refrigerator. The bathroom was fully adapted for handicapped residents, and there were grab bars next to where a bed logically fit. CC had the option of renting furnished or unfurnished. He opted for furnished, and Rose assured him, he would have furniture by tomorrow afternoon. The meal plan was required. Getting people up and out of their rooms was an important part of the daily routine. Studies had shown that people who moved and interacted with others had a better quality of life than their sedentary counterparts.

Each of the units faced a glass lined walkway to the Rec room and dining hall. No one had to get wet unless he went out his back door. A small patio door opened onto a tiny rectangle of cement shielded by a privacy fence on two sides. This door was fitted with a keyed deadbolt, and a button flashed at the nurse's station if the door were opened or remained open after dark. Residents could come and go as they pleased as long as they used the front doors with camera surveillance, but the patio doors were for emergencies only after the sun went down.

A small emergency occurred late Monday afternoon. Hattie West from the State Crime Lab called Marshall with an urgent message. Yes, the liquor was laced with arsenic, but it wasn't sherry. Based on contaminants, it appeared to be moonshine! Marshall immediately called Garnet, who immediately called Maynard. "Not to worry," Maynard reassured her. "I'll take care of it."

Maynard rummaged in the back corner under her kitchen sink and found the fruit jar that had been secreted three years ago. She had lifted it from George's room one night when he had drunk half of it and had fallen asleep in the floor beside his bed. His drinking had been the main cause of their divorce. She had learned years ago that she couldn't stop his drinking, but she could slow him down.

She poured the liquor into a large opaque travel cup and took it to Hannah, hoping she wasn't too late. The custom of drinking only in the late evening or at night was completely ignored by the residents who figured they'd just as well get their jollies when they could.

Hannah snuck back into Lettie's room and poured the sherry down the drain, replacing it with Maynard's moonshine. Where in the world was Lettie getting moonshine?

46

Monday night the moon was one day short of full. ADD and Beulah waited impatiently for it to get near its apex before starting out. ADD lived on the London end of 333 about 10 minutes from Augsburg. They didn't want to have to sit out there waiting for the moonstone's magic and possibly get noticed from the road.

Finally they started out. ADD had already loaded the truck with a pick and shovel, buckets and extra trash bags. Then he threw in some rope, just in case. They had needed it at Galley Rock. He drove slowly and turned left onto Augsburg Rd. at the sharp corner. He turned off the lights and steered the truck around to the back of the food pantry/community center. There, he turned the truck around so that it was facing out, just in case.

The two of them walked slowly down the paved incline to the last of three gates along the front fence line. This time it was Beulah who was carrying the shovel, and ADD was leading the way with the moonstone. The cemetery was neatly fenced with chain link fence around its entire perimeter, and the grass was neatly mowed between the long rows of grave stones. The straight rows of graves were laid out perpendicular to the front fence with the oldest stones, some back as far as 1885, located in the back three rows.

ADD took out the moonstone, turned his back to the moon, and looked into the stone's depths. Nothing. They moved nearer to the back corner toward the oldest part of the cemetery where Beulah was sure they should be. He cupped the stone in his hands and looked again. "Well, I'll be," he whispered. "There's something over there by that big stone." He led the way to a grave where the headstone was thoroughly worn by the elements. He took off his hunting cap to shield his little LED light. Gr..ta Bou....m..n. He turned off the light and returned to the moonstone. "This is it," he whispered to Beulah. "But I can't see any place to dig."

"Let me have a look," she muttered, getting down on her hands and knees. Slowly she crawled around the stone, searching the nooks and crannies with her hands. "Here it is!" she squealed loudly, eliciting a big shush from ADD. There was a small vase of artificial flowers at the front on a small, rectangular slab of rock. "This little doo-dad here moves," she informed him. "Hand me that planting trowel."

She dug around the rectangle carefully and lifted it just slightly with the trowel. "Oh, yeah," she spoke to no one in particular. "Come to Momma. Easy does it. I've got it!" She pulled out a slim package wrapped in black plastic and sealed with duct tape. She held it up for ADD to see, and he yanked it out of her hands in his excitement.

"Put that rock back. Let's get out of here," he instructed. "Hurry up!"

Beulah shoved the edge of the rectangle back under the front of the stone and positioned the small vase of flowers. "ADD, aren't you forgetting something?" she asked as he turned on his heel and started back.

ADD looked around, but didn't see anything amiss. "What?" he demanded gruffly.

"Me." She held out her hand for him to help her up. They walked as quickly as they could over the rocks and clods back to the food pantry and behind it to the truck. ADD put the truck in "creep" and they slowly returned to the main road. A right turn, and they were gone.

"What do you think it is, Addie?" Beulah asked. "It's got to be some kind of paper from the way it's wrapped. It's small enough it could be money, or maybe someone's will. What if it's a thousand dollars?"

"Well then, I reckon you'll find some place to spend it," he said dryly.

Their find tonight was not nearly so messy as the bag from Galley Rock. Beulah wiped it of with a wet paper towel and placed it on the table between them. ADD opened his pocket knife and carefully sliced through the duct tape to remove the outer layer. There was a second layer of black plastic sealed with duct tape. "This thing is getting' smaller," he commented. "Pretty soon there'll only be $500."

"At least whatever it is, it's dry," Beulah commented. "Somebody wanted that to last a long time."

ADD finally got the wrapping off, and there they were: three U.S. passports for Ella Justice, Howard Jackson, and Thelma Werner.

Monday night while CC and Pat were in bed, he said rather impetuously, "Run away with me, you beautiful creature."

"Oh, but of course I will," she responded laughingly.

"No, I'm serious. After all this Dimitri thing blows over, why don't we go down to the islands? We have plenty of money down there."

She realized he was half serious. "What about Rose?" she asked.

He shrugged his shoulders, "Rose can take care of herself. She probably has some place already picked out if I know her."

Pat changed the subject to his moving into his room. She had a gnawing feeling he knew something he wasn't telling her.

47

CC moved into his new digs with much fanfare and swaying. He made a point of introducing himself to everyone he came across. The men were cordial and offered to show him the outside premises when he was settled. The women were pleased that such a fine looking man had joined them. The ratio of women to men at this age was about four to one. Some of them invited him to after dinner drinks in their rooms, but he politely declined explaining in comical terms what alcohol did to his balancing system.

Pat promised to come see him Friday, giving him some time to get settled. The truth was that she needed to work in Ft. Smith Wednesday and Thursday. She had some prospects there she had been working to cultivate. Right now she had several stolen debit cards, but who knew when she might need a new identity in the future.

Rose was excited about having CC on the premises. She knew he'd make himself useful and suss out new prospective identities for them, although she already had a handle on the resident's finances based on their paperwork and their monthly billing. So far, she and Pat had gone for the low hanging fruit. There had to be people among the adjacent apartments and houses who had potential. She saw quite a few of them during Sunday's buffets, but there weren't many actual connections.

Rose was very pleased with herself this morning. She had stayed late last night looking for a conference for Hannah to attend. She had found just the one. The Association of Ambulatory Caregivers was having a conference this coming weekend in Tulsa. George Tanner was still in decline. If Rose could get Hannah to go away just Friday and Saturday night, George just might encounter some "natural causes".

Rose prepared herself for her performance and hurried down the hall to Hannah's office. "Oh, Hannah, look what I just came across. There's a conference this weekend in Tulsa for ambulatory caregivers. I know its short notice, but we can swing the late registration fee if you'd like to go. We should be able to get a reasonable room close by if the conference accommodations are sold out. What do you think?"

"Oh, I don't know," Hannah tried to act nonchalant even though she felt a surge of adrenalin. This was what they'd been waiting for. "I don't know that it'd help much. I could probably plan and present the conference myself. I've sure had lots of experience."

"I just thought you might like a weekend off on the house," Rose tried to sound neutral. "This would be a good way to find out if any new regulations are coming down the pike from the feds. It wouldn't hurt to have a heads-up for a change. Corporate has been really slow about letting us know any new requirements."

"Yeah, bless their hearts. I hate staying up all night filling out paperwork to meet their deadlines when a little notice would have been prudent on their part. Leave me the flyers, and I'll take a look. I'll get back to you by late afternoon."

Hannah called Rose back at 4:00. "You're right this could be a good conference. The Deputy Director for Regulatory Affairs from the National Agency on Aging will be there. I'd like to hear his speech."

Rose offered to make all the arrangements, and Hannah went home with an important piece of information to pass on to the CI.

Maynard had passed the information to Garnet, who passed it to Marshall. Garnet was excited and obsessed over possible scenarios. On her way home her mind ran through several "what ifs". What if Pat Lewis had the patches? Would she come in from the hallway or sneak in through the back? What if Rose came instead? What if a third, unnamed player came? Then there was the question of whether George should be moved. Probably not, since that would alert the murderer. Who would be watching? Where would law enforcement be stationed? Hopefully the people directly involved in the possible take-down had this all worked out.

Garnet was so preoccupied that she didn't see Uncle ADD's truck when she pulled in to the parking area. *Oh no! What now? What is he up to? Oh, rats. I forgot. It's a full moon tonight!* When Garnet opened her front door, there they were. Just like last month. The two of them were sitting at the big table chatting with Mica, and there was a package in the middle.

"Well, hi there," Garnet was pleasant in spite of herself. "This is a surprise. You've been out with that moonstone again, haven't you? What did you find this time?"

"I had another dream. Well actually I had several dreams, but you don't want to hear about Nancy Peolsi," Beulah was excited. This time it was Orville Faubus who sent us out. And I must say, his information was better than Jesse James'."

"Yep, I have to hand it to her," those dreams can be mighty helpful," ADD admitted. "We went up to the Zion Lutheran Cemetery at Augsburg, and it was right there," he pointed to the package.

"Another cemetery?" Garnet looked askance.

"Oh, yes," Beulah chimed in. We had to park around back of the church and sneak down to the cemetery, but there it was! The stone even had flowers marking it. You couldn't miss it. It was Greta Somebody. I think it was Boughman, but some of the letters were worn so you couldn't read them. I got down on my hands and knees and felt around. There was a little ledge at the front of the marker, and it moved! I dug down under it and found this envelope," she pointed to the package in the middle of the table. "We couldn't wait to get home to open it!"

"Well, we know what it is, but we don't know what it means," ADD explained. "So we brought it to you since one of the names is the same."

One of which names? Garnet wondered.

"Go ahead and open it," Beulah instructed. "It's not nearly as scary as the last time."

Garnet signaled to Mica that he should open it. He picked it up gingerly and shook it just a little. No noise. Then he peeled off the waterproof layers and laid out three U.S. passports, one for Ella Justice, one for Howard Jackson, and one for an unknown woman, Thelma Werner.

"Well, well, well, the plot thickens," Mica offered.

"You're right," Garnet addressed the other two. "Ella Justice was one of the names on the boxes of cremains. Her lost or stolen passport being found in a different cemetery adds to the mystery. I'll take these in to the sheriff's office tomorrow. Their detective, Marshall Boggs, will surely want to see these. Would you like to stay for supper? I can rustle up something pretty easily."

"No, no," ADD was firm. We got things to do tonight. Some other time, Garner, Honey."

"You don't fool me, you old rascal," she returned. You're going out with that moonstone again, aren't you?"

"You bet. We've been to two cemeteries and found two hauls. There's no tellin' what's buried out there. Tonight we're goin' up to the Pollard Cemetery!"

48

Wednesday night after her shift, Pat called CC just to reinforce their new intimacy. It took several rings before he answered, then he mumbled into the phone. He said the day had gone well, and he was actually getting ready for bed. That was when she heard the woman giggle. But it wasn't just any woman. It was Rose! Pat's deja vu told her immediately that wherever they were, either at Golden Rod Acres, or more probably at Rose's, they were planning to have sex. Pat had always known they couldn't be trusted together, and she also knew they were consenting adults. Still it bothered her. It bothered her a lot. Maybe it was because she'd been alone for so long, but she had let herself buy into the fantasy of moving with CC to a Caribbean island for a semiretirement. Worse, she had actually been looking forward to it.

Thursday was an important day for Marshall. He was anxious to talk to Sue Kochner in Personnel at Jewish Hospital in St. Louis. He watched the clock until the appointed time. Ms. Kochner picked up right away.

"Well, I have found out several things for you," she said cheerfully. "I was able to get the old records printed out. Let me see. Oh yes, Rose Cassidy was the head administrative assistant for the Gastroenterology group. Patricia Lewis was an RN for the group, and Thelma Werner was an RN in Oncology."

Thelma Werner at last. Let's see if we can find out more about her. "Do you know if Thelma and Patricia knew each other?"

"Yes, I looked up the woman who was head administrative assistant for Gastroenterology back then. She remembered all three of them as good friends. Lunch together, exchanging shifts, and so on. That is until the tragedy."

Marshall's ears pricked up, "the tragedy?"

"Oh, evidently it was a scandal at the time. Rose Cassidy committed suicide. They found her in her office when the early shift came in."

"Can you tell me how she did it?" he prompted.

Well, according to the administrative assistant, she OD'd on fentanyl. She had several high dosage patches on her body, so I guess there wasn't any pain. Still..."

"What happened to the ladies then?" he continued to fish.

Well, according to the office manager, Thelma Werner left right away. I guess Rose's death plus the high death rate in Oncology was too much for her."

"What about Patricia Lewis?"

"Her records show she stayed another year."

"Do you know where either woman went?"

"No idea."

"Did you learn anything else about Rose from the administrative assistant?"

"Well, there was one thing. She said she never saw three women who loved chocolate so much. They were always having chocolate parties at Rose's desk on breaks or at lunch. And, they shared with anyone who wanted to come. Sometimes there'd be six or eight people up there."

"Marshall had a sudden idea. "One last thing, do you, or did you have a physician named Roberta Halston?"

Ms. Kochner checked an alphabetical listing of both old and new employees. "No," she said. "Her name isn't on the list."

After the call, Marshall looked up the personnel records for Rose Cassidy and Pat Lewis. Both women had used Dr. Halston as a reference. Out of curiosity he called the number penciled in by her name and called it. The number was no longer in service.

So, Thelma Werner, AKA Rose Cassidy was a nurse. Maybe she didn't need another nurse to put those fentanyl patches on. Was it possible that Pat Lewis was innocent and was being used?

Pat's plan had been almost instantaneous when she recognized Rose's laugh over the phone. She told CC she'd stop by his room Thursday night late, after her shift. That way she was sure Rose would be out of the way when she confronted him. During the night Wednesday, she thought about loyalty and options. Then just before she left Ft. Smith Thursday, she placed an anonymous call to the FBI, letting them know where they could find Pierre Brevard/Carson Kellog. She drove across the Arkansas River heading west just so she could throw her burner phone off the bridge. That way, if the feds pinged her, they'd believe the call came from Ft. Smith.

She cut off at London on her way back to Russellville and made her way to Augsburg. Like ADD and Beulah, she parked behind the community building at the Lutheran Church then made her way on foot to the cemetery. She carried a small flashlight, and with the full moon's light, easily made it to the familiar tombstone of Greta Boughman. She shut off her light and knelt to slide the rectangular rock away from the front. Shock! Nothing there! She turned her light on and dug around some more. Still nothing. This turn of events helped strengthen her resolve to carry out her plan.

Pat skipped the trip out to Golden Rod Acres, heading straight for her apartment. Let CC stew. He couldn't pester her on the phone unless he wanted to take a dip into the Arkansas River. He'd get his tomorrow. When she arrived, she called Rose and said she was back. Rose invited her over for drinks later. Pat agreed to drinks in about an hour, then began packing for a long trip.

It was already 10:00 when Pat knocked on Rose's door, but they were used to these late night "business meetings". They'd been drinking together over their business plans for years. Assuming someone else's identity took some planning even if you were good at it. They talked a lot about George Tanner and drank several Margaritas. They agreed on Friday night well after dark as the time to attack using the usual fentanyl patches. They nailed down a few other details then celebrated by drinking a few more Margaritas. When Rose went to the bathroom, Pat added a few drops of ketamine to Rose's drink.

It didn't take long for Rose, who was already woozy, to sag more and more on her couch until she was almost lying down as she fell asleep. Pat put on gloves then went into Rose's bedroom to hide three 100mg fentanyl patches in her luggage in the closet. Then she quickly placed three patches across Rose's chest. Finally she dropped a pen and paper onto the coffee table (she was very good at forgery by now). The note simply said, "Carson, I am so sorry. Please...". Pat thought the unfinished note was a stroke of genius.

49

Friday was both an exciting and a disappointing day. By the end of the day, things had not gone as planned.

The first unusual thing was that Rose did not show up for work. She didn't call in sick, and her phone went to voice mail. That wasn't a problem until the two FBI agents showed up asking for Carson Kellog. Nobody had a clue, and Rose's resident records were locked up. But when the agents asked to see any men who had moved in during the past two months, Gracie was able to help. Two months ago, Mr. Simon had moved in, and just this week, Mr. Charles Ballard had joined the group. She gave them the room numbers and directed them down the hall.

Imagine the surprise of the residents who were sitting calmly listening to Maynard's pre-lunch serenade when the two agents came through the Rec room literally dragging a reluctant Mr. Ballard. Not only was he reluctant, but he was also vocal. "Call Rose Cassidy! She'll tell you who I am! This is preposterous (and other bits of useless trivia)," shouted at the top of his lungs. Maynard was so startled that she began playing the Marines Hymn without thinking. Later the others commented that it was a truly suitable accompaniment.

Hannah left for Tulsa about 1:00. She wanted to be here tonight, but knew calmly carrying out the planned schedule was important. She drove the three and one-half hours to Tulsa and checked into her motel before she went to the convention venue. As soon as she had registered, she drove back to Muskogee for dinner with Randi.

When mother and daughter met at Applebees, Hannah could tell Randi had something important to tell her (*oh no, not a wedding*). But that wasn't even close. Randi had sent her DNA off to a site and had marked the permission to share box. Guess what? Someone from southern Oklahoma had contacted her. Twenty-five per cent of their DNA matched, almost enough to be siblings! She was going to drive down to Durant tomorrow to meet this genetic relative. And, guess what? He wasn't Seminole. He was Quapaw!

Hannah was so bumfuzzled she had trouble responding. Not that Randi's DNA had anything to do with her, but the girl had been hyping the Seminoles since she was five years old. Now she was saying she was Quapaw. These new people could be anything. They could be dirt poor, or worse, they could be rich. How would she and Randi deal with that? She reminded herself again, *it's not about me; it's not about me.* She just hoped Randi wouldn't give too much emotionally and get hurt.

Hannah had kissed Randi goodbye and started up HWY-59 to pick up the Muskogee Turnpike back to Tulsa when the little voice she had been ignoring all day finally broke through. She needed to go home. She turned right at the ramp and headed back to Arkansas.

It was almost midnight when she eased her car into a space out of sight of the facility. She walked north, then east past Maynard's, keeping to the tree line. She took her stethoscope out of her bag and entered the back door as if she were on duty. She almost panicked when one of the nurses' aides stopped her in the glassed in hallway. "Oh, hi Hannah," she seemed relieved somehow, "that Pat nurse never showed up. I guess they called you to come back from Tulsa."

Hannah smiled and asked, "any problems so far?"

"No," the night aide replied. "But its good to know you're here if we need you."

Hannah went on down the hall as if she were making her rounds. Then she ducked into George's darkened room. He was asleep on his back, snoring loudly. She pushed him onto his side and sat down in the dark to wait.

She had almost dozed off when she heard someone at the back door trying to get a key into the lock. She started pumping adrenalin as she slipped out of the chair and crawled toward the foot of the bed. She had brought an LED lantern from the trunk of her car, and she was ready for action. The scraping at the door stopped. Instead she heard Maynard's high pitched scream, "you can't have him! You can't have him! He's mine I tell you. He's mine, and you're not taking him from me."

Hannah heard bumping and banging in the small patio as she used her key to open the dead bolt. She turned on her lantern to see a large man dressed only in black with Maynard riding his back. He was trying to rub her off, and she was hanging on for dear life. She had managed to pull his knit cap off and her hands were buried in his hair. As he turned toward Hannah with his kicking and screaming attacker, Hannah hit his face with the light. She couldn't believe it. Leon!

Just then Marshall and another officer burst on the scene with pistols drawn. Leon threw his arms up in surrender, and Hannah went over to pull a hysterical Maynard off his back. She turned the light back toward his face and burst out angrily, "so you're the one who murdered Ella Justice and the others. Maynard's right. You're not getting George Tanner!"

He melted on the spot. "Murder? You think I murdered someone? No. No. You've got it wrong. I never hurt anyone. I swear!"

"What's that in your backpack?" Marshall pointed to where the pack had been kicked into the corner. The other officer retrieved it, and they marched back around the corner into the front door of the Rec room for better light. Inside were three pint sized drinking bottles with screw on lids. Marshall opened one and sniffed cautiously. Then he passed the bottle around to the others who all took a sniff. Moonshine!

"Did you lace this with arsenic?" Marshall was angry at the large man.

"Arsenic?" Leon's eyes grew big as saucers. "Is that why my stomach has been killing me lately?"

"Depends on how much you've been drinking," Marshall was not encouraging. In the back of his mind he remembered that Leon had DUIs from Texarkana. "Who've you been selling it to?"

"Oh, just a couple of my friends, and here at Golden Rod. I sell to George and Ettie mostly. Moonshine's an acquired taste, you know."

"Leon, there are three bottles. Who is the other one for?"

"I usually give one to Miss Rose," he answered sheepishly.

50

Leon's arrest Friday night raised more questions than it answered. Was Leon the source of the arsenic laced moonshine? If so, was it deliberate on his part? Why had Rose not come to work Friday? Had she tipped the feds to Carson Kellog? The FBI agents had been pretty mum as expected, but they did reveal that he was wanted as a known associate of Dimitri Popolov. What was Carson's, or Dimitri's for that matter, connection to Rose and/or Pat Lewis?

Leon was in bad shape. He continued to throw up during the night, either from arsenic or from fright. By morning the distinct smell of vomit permeated the air in his cell. When he wasn't puking his guts out, he was sniveling about his innocence. It was so bad that none of the officers wanted to do a cell check. It was a good thing he wasn't suicidal or he might have been successful.

One of Marshall's assistants was waiting at the State Crime Lab in Dardanelle when lab director Hattie West herself came in on a Saturday to test the moonshine for arsenic. It didn't take long for the results. The test was positive.

Now Leon was really in a mess. He told his jailors over and over that he had not poisoned the shine. Yes, he had been sick at his stomach off and on for about a month. And no, he had no idea who might have poisoned the liquor. To make matters worse, when he learned about the positive test for arsenic, he believed he was on death's door, and his dry heaves and sniveling worsened.

Since neither Rose nor Pat Lewis had appeared, Marshall took two officers and went to their apartments. The landlord gave them a key and pointed to a map of the layout of the complex, pointing out the two locations. As soon as they entered Pat's apartment, it was clear to them that Pat had cleared out. The place was neat as a pin with empty closets, empty drawers, and empty trash. On the little kitchen table they found a driver's license, a credit card, a bank book, and a debit card, all with the name Patricia Lewis. It was as if she had left that person, or rather that identity, behind.

Rose's apartment was a lot messier. A very dead Rose was lying in the tight space between the couch and the coffee table. A half consumed Margarita sat on the table, and a hand written note was on the carpet. The kitchen was too clean for the rest of the scene, suggesting someone else may have been drinking with her. A thorough search of the apartment turned up two unopened bottles of tequila and three unlabeled fentanyl patches hidden in luggage.

51

This was a prosecutor's nightmare. There was plenty of evidence that identity theft and even murder had occurred. But there wasn't enough evidence to prosecute any specific person or persons.

There was no hard evidence that Leon had added the arsenic to the moonshine. A search of his apartment and the shop at work was fruitless. He still had five jars of liquor, but only two of them tested positive for arsenic. And it was unclear how long the liquor poisoning had been going on. Ettie's symptoms suggested less than a month of poisoning. But George had continued to have symptoms even after the chocolate had been switched. Was his poisoning chocolate and moonshine, or first chocolate then moonshine? Leon admitted he had been slipping both George and Ettie "a little something" for over a year, but neither had sickened until the last two months. Why now? Why not a year ago?

And, importantly, what was the source of the fentanyl patches? And, why were they always applied when Pat Lewis was on duty? They had assumed that Pat Lewis, being a nurse, had applied the patches. But Marshall had discovered that Thelma Werner, AKA Rose Cassidy was a nurse too. Had she put the patches on with Pat standing by to fill out the death certificates?

Following the money had proved to be quite difficult. Over $100 thousand dollars had vanished into cashiers checks. Where was it now? The evidence was clear that Rose Cassidy had written the checks out of the victim's accounts. Or had she? Pat could have forged names as easily as Rose. It was clearly a case of theft and theft by receiving.

And where was the wily Pat? Dressed in an elegant emerald green blouse with a beautiful, truly unique, gemmed elk's tooth fastened to the collar, and driving a brand new Lexus, she was headed back east to Indiana with the cashiers checks, several stolen credit and debit cards, and three new identities. She had manufactured, rather than stolen, the one she was using now. Today Patricia Lewis, AKA any number of past identities, was none other than Greta Boughman.

The End

www.ingramcontent.com/pod-product-compliance
Lightning Source LLC
Chambersburg PA
CBHW051128260626
47170CB00005B/1721